GW01418510

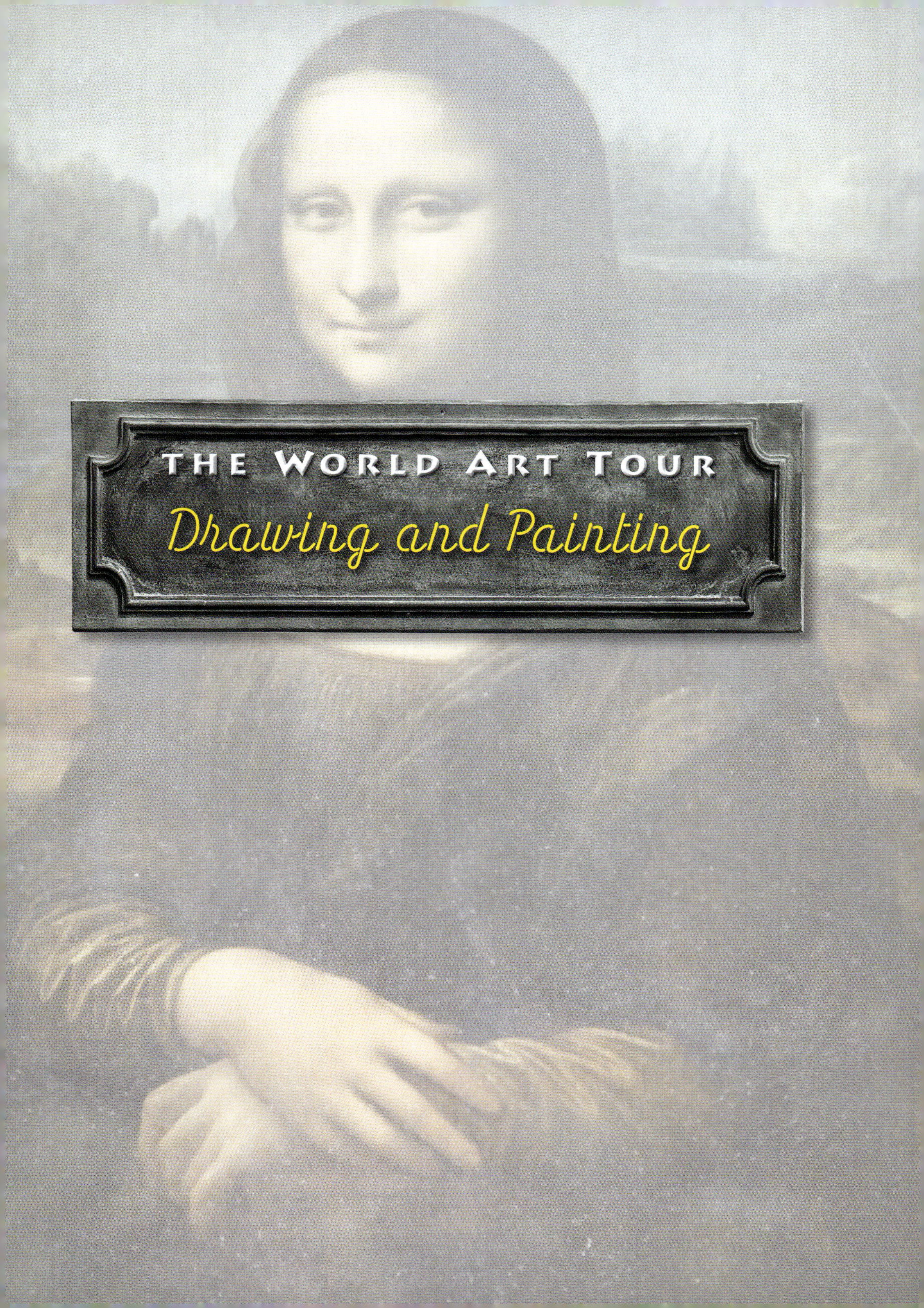

The World Art Tour

Drawing and Painting

Architecture

Clothing and Fashion

Culinary Arts

Dance

Decorative Arts

Drawing and Painting

Festivals

Sculpture

THE WORLD ART TOUR
Drawing and Painting

BY Christina Wedberg

MC

MASON CREST
Philadelphia • Miami

Mason Crest
450 Parkway Drive, Suite D
Broomall, PA 19008
(866) MCP-BOOK (toll free)
www.masoncrest.com

Copyright © 2020 by Mason Crest, an imprint of National Highlights, Inc. All rights reserved. No part of this publication may be reproduced or transmitted in any form or by any means, electronic or mechanical, including photocopying, recording, taping, or any information storage and retrieval system, without permission in writing from the publisher.

Printed in the United States of America

First printing
9 8 7 6 5 4 3 2 1

Series ISBN: 978-1-4222-4283-4
Hardcover ISBN: 978-1-4222-4289-6
ebook ISBN: 978-1-4222-7536-8

Cataloging-in-Publication Data is available on file
at the Library of Congress.

Developed and Produced by Print Matters Productions, Inc.
(www.printmattersinc.com)

Cover and Interior Design by Tom Carling, Carling Design, Inc.

CONTENTS

INTRODUCTION

The history of drawing and painting stretches back to the dawn of humanity. People were drawing pictures before they knew how to write words. The earliest known drawings, found in South Africa, date back around 73,000 years. Drawings can be works of art, but more than that, they express human emotion in the most profound and simple way. They symbolize the first step in an idea of the imagination that can grow from the seed of a sketch into the full bloom of a painting.

Like all art forms, drawing and painting have evolved throughout time and history. Each new art movement around the world has come from the inspiration of the art movements that came before it. As time has passed, drawing and painting styles have changed, as have the art materials people have used. In African art, drawing and painting expressed people's respect for nature, their culture, and the delicate balance between life and death. The ancient Egyptians drew hieroglyphs and painted on the walls of tombs in pyramids to help send off the deceased to the afterlife.

THE INVENTION OF PAPER

The process of making paper is thought to have begun in China sometime in the second century CE. Before the invention of paper, the Chinese used canvases of silk to create their ink drawings and paintings. The process of making paper soon spread throughout the Middle East and Europe.

In Europe, modern drawing began during the Renaissance in the 1400s. The use of drawing and painting on paper became more common, because paper was easier to obtain. Drawing was soon considered to be the foundation for all other arts. Art students who were beginning studies in art had to first master drafting skills before they could go on to learn painting or sculpture. Art students also carefully studied nature and learned to draw what they saw in terms of physical structure and anatomy, often by drawing nude models. In this way, artists' depictions of the human figure became more and more realistic over time.

During the Renaissance, many European artists used preparatory drawing to work on their paintings. For example, large-scale paintings that were to be created in churches or other public buildings required an extensive amount of preparation, and drawings were an important step in that process. Artists used pen and ink to draw, but they also experimented with chalks and charcoal in red and black colors. They began incorporating shading and texture in drawing and paintings. Some of the greatest draftsmen of this time were Leonardo da Vinci and Michelangelo.

In Latin America and the Caribbean region, the roots of drawing and painting have their origins among the many different indigenous cultures that inhabited these lands, as well as the influences of European colonizers who came to discover the treasures of these countries.

PORTRAYING CULTURE AND TRADITION

In the Middle Eastern art world, calligraphy was and is still a highly esteemed and sophisticated art form that has been intertwined with drawing and painting for hundreds of years. In Middle Eastern countries such as Israel, Syria, and Palestine, artists continue to evolve and grow their artistic styles in sometimes violent and challenging circumstances.

Long before the colonists landed in the Americas, Native American peoples had been drawing and painting as an integral part of their cultures and traditions. Over time, the European settlers of North America forged their own styles in art. From the whimsical folk art of traveling artists to innovative comic book and magazine illustrators, each art movement found its own individual style.

The art of Oceania is shared by the aboriginal peoples of New Zealand and Australia, as well as the colonists who came to settle in this new and wild landscape, looking for a better life. The aboriginal peoples of this region had many ways of using drawing and painting as a way to celebrate their culture, including body painting, facial tattoos, and rock art.

THE MODERN ERA

Drawing made significant advances in the 1800s when pencils began to be manufactured. For many artists, pencils became the preferred drawing tool, but others experimented with various media, such as brush with black and gray washes, oil on paper, pastels, and crayons. Artists like Edgar Degas experimented with these media to create representations of everyday scenes, such as ballet dancers practicing or a day at the horse races. By the end of the 1800s, however, artists began to question the traditional academic training and practice of drawing. During the Impressionist movement, artists rejected making a preliminary drawing and painted directly on the canvas.

Since the start of the twentieth century, the world of painting and drawing has taken a direction away from past traditions and attempted to forge a new voice for each individual artist. The meaning of drawing and painting has thus evolved and expanded. So now more than ever, drawing or painting can be anything an artist desires. This idea can be found in a myriad of new and emerging art movements, such as comic book and magazine illustration, manga art, and street art.

KEY TERMS

Abstract: Art that depicts shapes and forms that are not easily recognized as people, animals, or natural objects.

Allegorical: A symbolic representation that has a hidden or spiritual meaning distinct from the literal form.

Atmospheric: Something that contributes to an emotional or aesthetic impression or tone.

Constructivism: An art movement that originated in Russia in the 1920s. The main idea was the sorting of mechanical objects into abstract structural forms.

Cubism: Created by Pablo Picasso and Georges Braque in the early 20th century. This movement rejected the idea of perspective and foreshortening and emphasized flat, two-dimensional surface planes.

Culture: A set of beliefs, customs, attitudes, values, and goals that are shared by a group or people.

Diaspora: A population of people who have been scattered to geographic locations outside of their homeland.

Embellishment: An ornamentation or decorative detail that is added to something to make it more interesting or attractive.

Encaustic: Hot wax mixed in with a pigment that is burnt into something, such as wood or canvas, and used as an inlay.

Fauvism: A movement of early twentieth century artists that emphasized a use of strong color and painterly qualities with a loose-brush technique.

Figurative: A way of representing forms in artwork that are easily recognizable in real life.

Foreshortening: A method of rendering an object with depth that creates the illusion of the object receding into the distance or appearing shorter than it really is.

Fresco: Painting that is done rapidly on wet plaster or in watercolor, usually on a ceiling or a wall, so that the colors of the paint soak in to the plaster and become permanent.

Fringe: Not part of the mainstream of thinking; extreme or unconventional.

Futurism: An art movement that originated in Italy in the early twentieth century. The emphasis was on casting away older forms of culture and embracing speed, youth, change, technology, and violence.

Hieroglyph: A picture of an object that represents a word or a sound. Hieroglyphs are highly stylized and often found in ancient Egyptian writing.

Iconic: An object of devotion that can be a religious image or a person. It is typically painted on a small panel made of wood.

Illuminated: To decorate or embellish a page or the first initial of a letter in a manuscript. It can be decorated with gold, silver, or other colored designs.

Impressionism: An art movement that started in France in the 1860s. It was characterized by depicting an image at a specific moment in time, such as the shifting light on a lake.

Indigenous: An ethnic group comprising the first people or original inhabitants of a certain geographic location.

Modernism: An artistic and philosophical movement that sought to break free from traditional and classical forms and ideas.

Neoclassical: Western artistic movements that drew their inspiration from the classical tradition and aesthetic of ancient Greece and Rome.

Ocher: A kind of pigment made from the earth that contains ferric oxide and clay. The color can vary from red to light yellow or brown.

Paradoxical: A statement that seems true but ends up leading to a self-contradiction or an unacceptable conclusion.

Pastoral: An idealized representation of the countryside that is pleasing, innocent, and peaceful.

Perspective: A technique the represents a plane or surface in relation to other objects as they might appear to the eye that gives them the illusion of depth.

Plein air: A painting technique that involves working outdoors to capture the natural light and air in the artwork.

Proportionality: The way that objects correspond in size, shape, and intensity.

Rationalism: A belief that an opinion or theory should be based on reason, logic, and knowledge, rather than on an emotional or religious reaction.

Repertoire: A list or a range of skills or a collection of things that are regularly performed.

Rococo: A highly ornamental style of decoration that began in the 1730s. This style used pastel colors, scrolls, gilding, and frescoes to create an air of motion and drama.

Symbolism: A way of using symbols to represent an idea, quality, or meaning or to express an emotion or a certain state of mind.

Zoomorphic: A Greek word that means "form" or "shape." It can mean representing one kind of animal like another kind of animal. It can also mean imagining a human as an animal.

Africa is a rich and majestic land with a history as old as time. From apartheid art, African landscapes, and fantasy coffins to the world's oldest drawings found in Blombos Cave near Cape Town, Africa has long been a place where art and creativity meld into the life, culture, and traditions of its people.

PAINTINGS OF ANCIENT EGYPT

Egyptian art comes from a civilization that dates back around 5,000 years, from approximately 3000 BCE to 30 CE. Remarkably, because of the dry climate of this region, this art remained in very good condition for millennia, sitting safely inside the tombs of the pharaohs. This artwork was never meant to be seen by anyone. It was intended only for the pharaohs to enjoy in the afterlife, as they would hunting or fishing.

The ancient Egyptians used their artistic skills to make beautiful and elaborate tombs for their pharaohs. The pyramids were built to be used as tombs for the pharaohs and other royalty. They created a number of spectacular paintings inside these tombs, depicting scenes such as the journey of the deceased in the afterlife. Other painted scenes in each tomb depict the life events and activities of that particular pharaoh while he was alive, so that he could enjoy them again after death. Some scenes also include paintings of protective deities introducing the pharaoh to Osiris, the god of the underworld.

Egyptians painted the inside of tombs with gods and hieroglyphics.

A scroll from the Egyptian Book of the Dead.

The paintings of ancient Egypt were created on several different kinds of surfaces inside the tombs. Some were painted on stone that was prepared with a whitewash or a layer of coarse plaster. Then a second layer of gesso was applied and allowed to dry before the artist began his painting. Other surfaces, such as limestone, could be painted on directly, with no undersurface needed for the paint.

The pigments for the paints were mostly made up of naturally occurring minerals. It is not known what binding medium was used, perhaps egg tempera or an assortment of resins and gums. The main colors used for paintings were black, yellow, red, blue, gold, and green. Black paint was made from carbon, red and yellow paint from iron oxide, white from gypsum, and blue and green paint from azurite. After a painting was finished, a varnish was usually applied to protect it.

The perspective of most paintings was taken from a profile view and a side view of a subject, such as a person or animal. In other words, people would be depicted with their body facing front but their head facing to the side. In addition, most paintings did not feature a sense of depth but rather focused on a two-dimensional surface. The figures varied in size according to their importance, and a king would often be the same size as a god.

Scenes in a painting would be ordered in parallel lines called registers. Each register separated the scene and provided a base or ground line for the subject of the painting. Scenes without a register were meant to represent chaos or disorder and featured subjects such as battles or hunting scenes, with the prey or a fallen army without a ground line. Registers also conveyed the importance of a scene. The higher up the scene on a register, the higher the status of the subject.

Text, in the form of hieroglyphs, was important in Egyptian art, too, and would almost always accompany a painting. During the New Kingdom period (c. 1550–1070 BCE) and after, the *Book of the Dead* was buried with the deceased. This book was considered important because it was an introduction to the afterlife.

BODY PAINTING

People in Africa have been decorating their bodies with paint for thousands of years, and some cultures continue this tradition to this day. Body painting is one of the oldest art forms in Africa, and early evidence of its beginnings date back 4,000–7,000 years. In Chad, cave paintings have been found of the Niola Doa, or "Beautiful Ladies," who are decorated in body paint from head to toe.

Among some cultures in Africa, a human being's skin is regarded as a blank canvas that can, and should, be decorated. Body painting can be used to represent a person's social status or religious beliefs. It was first used to contact the spirit world, to distinguish between those who were tribe members and those who were enemies, or to attract the opposite sex.

Some cultures use body paint only for important social occasions, but some cultures use body paint every day to signify individuals' social status. Still other cultures have abandoned the social and religious significance of body painting and participate in decorating their bodies merely as a show for tourists, as a way to make a living in the modern world.

The colors that are used in body painting vary from tribe to tribe. The kinds of materials that are used also vary, and can include chalk, ash, fruit, or sap to make

Two boys from the Karo tribe paint their faces.

the paint for different colors and textures. Since the late nineteenth century, some tribes have begun to use commercially made paint, rather than make it from naturally occurring minerals.

In Sudan, Nuba males paint and decorate their bodies from the ages of 17 to 30 to indicate what stage of life they are in. Among the Nuba peoples, the kinds of designs and colors that are used for body paint depend on strict religious and social guidelines for each specific tribe. For example, the color white can be used for both boys and girls in religious rituals that initiate them into their society. Colors can then be added to the body paint repertoire according to the person's stage of life. A young Nuba man can wear the colors red and white from the time that he is eight years old, but he has to wait until he is older to wear yellow paint. Further, he cannot wear the color black until he is initiated into the tribe as a full member. The young women of Nuba coat their bodies with red ocher and oil to signify the time between puberty and their first pregnancy.

In Ethiopia, body painting is also used to celebrate each stage of a person's life. Different colors and patterns are used, depending on the tribe. For example, the color red can signify happiness and life, but it can also signify death and sadness. The Omo River people use body chalk. The Himba Pastoralists from Namibia and the Maasai people of Kenya cover their bodies in red ocher. The color red symbolizes the life force. In West Africa, voodoo worshipers cover their bodies in a white powder called kaolin that is considered "food for the gods." It is meant to entice a deity to enter a person's body and empower him or her.

Members of the Omo River people.

APARTHEID ART

In South Africa, the liberation struggle movement (or "liberation movement") lasted from the 1960s to the 1990s. Initially, the State saw this movement as a benefit, because it would prove the government's success at separating the races into two separate environments. But as the movement grew exponentially and influenced greater numbers of people, the State reacted violently. In the arts, this meant enforced censorship and strict control of art displays and cultural institutions.

A number of schools of thought were formed during this time in an effort to express people's protest against the racial oppression of the authoritarian South African government. One movement wanted to use art as a weapon to express political opinions to come together as a community. Some artists felt that they could not deny the reality of living in an oppressive society, and they believed their art needed to reflect the injustices of state repression. The artists of the liberation struggle wanted to create a new revolutionary culture.

An event that was viewed as a catalyst during this time was the Sharpeville massacre of 1960, in which 69 people were killed and 180 others injured during an apartheid protest. It is seen as one of the most important turning points in the history of South Africa, and it highlighted the growing divide between white and black South Africans.

This painting, by Godfrey Rubens, depicts the Sharpeville massacre.

The art that was created during the apartheid era expressed criticism toward the State's political, cultural, and racial policies and was labeled "resistance art." Some artists chose to express their support for the struggle of South African blacks openly to mobilize the people. Others did not overtly support resistance art but still wanted to represent the impact of the norms of the society during this time.

By the early 1980s, many artists were tackling racial issues and violence head on, using stark and gory images that represented the real-life events of the day. In response to the killing of resistance leaders such as Bantu Steve Biko, an artist named Paul Stopforth created a series of paintings that dealt with the subject of police torture and brutality. Other artists, including Robert Hodgins, used satire paintings to protest against figures of power. Helen Sebidi used pastels, charcoals, and collages to express the struggle of human life, with figures battling in an upward motion as though they were drowning. Still other anonymous artists protested apartheid by posting stickers or posters of images of violence at traffic intersections.

Helen Sebidi's art (right) is featured in London museums.

THE FANTASTIC COFFINS OF GHANA

In Ghana, West Africa, the death of a person is considered a transition to the spirit realm of the ancestors. Ancestors are considered members of the extended family, and if the deceased are honored properly at their funeral, it is believed this will bring good favor upon the remaining living family left on earth.

Fantasy coffin makers make caskets for families because they believe that their loved one will continue his or her profession in the afterlife. Families request a fantasy coffin for a deceased loved one with the notion that the deceased person will remember where they came from and the family they left behind. Painted with bright colors, these coffins can be made to symbolize a person's main character trait, their standing in the community, their occupation, or something that they hope to acquire in the afterlife. Caskets can be made in the form of almost anything, from buildings, cars, and ships to animals or bananas.

Fantasy coffin makers like Joseph Ashong, also known as Paa Joe, take their business seriously. Paa Joe has been making coffins for more than 50 years. He

The fantasy coffins of Ghana are made to reflect a person's standing in the community, their occupation, or what they hope to achieve in the afterlife.

Fantasy coffin makers take their work very seriously.

started as an apprentice to his uncle when he was 15 and has been making coffins ever since. For local people, Paa Joe charges around $1,000 because he can use cheaper materials. However, for international clients, he may charge anywhere from $5,000 to $15,000 per coffin because international standards for making a coffin require a high-grade hardwood such as mahogany to protect against cracking and insects. A coffin typically takes him about two weeks to produce, and he will paint it with bright colors to resemble whatever object it is meant to be.

Fantasy coffin makers typically make seven or eight coffins per month. There are about eight to ten fantasy coffin makers living in the Accra region of Ghana. The National Museum of Funeral History in Houston, Texas, has the largest collection of fantasy coffins outside of Ghana, and images of many of them can be viewed on the museum's Web site (https://www.nmfh.org/).

CHRISTIAN ART OF ETHIOPIA

Christianity in Ethiopia dates back to the fourth century CE, when the kingdom of Aksum was located along the international trade route between the Roman Empire and India. Scientists believe that Christianity spread to Ethiopia when King Ezana was converted in the beginning of the fourth century. The Church of the Redeemer, the largest church in Lalibela, has interiors that are covered with paintings and murals of various saints performing miracles or acts of bravery. One example is a colorful mural of St. George riding on his horse and slaying a dragon.

The Early Solomonic period (1270–1530) was a time where royal churches were established and decorated with lavish wall paintings, such as the churches

The paintings in Gondar churches cover much of the walls and ceilings.

Detail from one of the Gondar church paintings.

of Lasta and Tigray. Royal patrons recruited European artists to paint artwork to enhance the prestige of these new churches. Through this patronage, Ethiopian artists were exposed to new media and artistic styles, and they used this knowledge to incorporate different ideas into their own individual works. Some of the new techniques included a shift from only front-facing portraits to three-quarter poses. They also began to use geometric patterning to create more three-dimensional figures.

Many images of Jesus's mother Mary were painted as icons, and she became an important figure in the Ethiopian church. During the Islamic jihads of 1531–1543, many churches were destroyed in Ethiopia, but some examples of patronage paintings from the period were saved by being hidden in monasteries that were extremely remote.

Churches that were built in the city of Gondar are entirely covered with paintings that were commissioned by wealthy patrons, because it was thought that it would give them a better place in heaven. Many of these paintings were devoted to icons of Mary and other saints.

Between the thirteenth and fifteenth centuries, churches such as Gannata Maryam near Lalibela were carved directly out of the rock, and the walls were painted with murals of angels, saints, and scenes inspired by the New Testament. There were also many manuscripts with illuminated illustrations that depicted the saints and pictures of the Virgin Mary with the infant Jesus. During this time, panel paintings of icons were used in church rituals.

In the Gondarine period (1632–1769), there were two phases of artistic styles in painting. The first style used bright colors with very little emphasis on shading. The clothing of people depicted in portraits was decorated with flourishes and painted in bright colors of blue, yellow, and red, with simple parallel lines to indicate folds in the clothing. The faces were painted in a plain coral red that led to an unnatural-looking appearance. The second Gondarine style (1730–1755) used darker colors and contour lines to provide a bit more shading and dimension to the bodies and faces of the portraits. Many paintings of this time were portraits of patrons and donors.

EMERGING CONTEMPORARY AFRICAN ART AND ARTISTS

Emerging contemporary African artists continue to pave the way for future artists by blending the culture and traditions of the past and present.

Julie Mehretu, born in Ethiopia, is an important African artist in her generation. Her paintings are large-scale, energetic pieces that represent accelerated urban growth and city environments. She creates her paintings by using many thin layers of acrylic paint on her canvas, and she finishes each piece with fragile patterns and marks by using pen, pencil, ink, and wisps of paint. She describes her work as "story maps of no location," and it can be classified as a combination of Geometric Abstraction, Constructivism, and Futurism.

Ibrahim el-Salahi is considered the godfather of African Modernism. His style is a mix of Surrealism with African and Arab influences. He was one of the first artists in Africa to incorporate Arabic calligraphy into his paintings. In his early work, his themes highlighted simplistic forms and lines. Over time, his work has evolved to continue the theme of elementary form and line but with a more abstract form in black and white colors. During the 1970s, el-Salahi served as a diplomat and under-secretary of the Sudanese Ministry of Culture. He was accused of antigovernment activities and imprisoned for six months without being charged in 1975.

Chéri Samba is a contemporary African painter who expresses his perception of daily life in his home of the Democratic Republic of the Congo. Samba started out as a billboard painter and then turned to painting on sacking fabric because canvas was too expensive. He is known for the "word bubbles" that are incorporated into his art, which allow him to include commentary in his paintings. They are known as the "Samba signature."

Ibrahim el-Salahi stands in front of his painting Reborn Sounds of Childhood Dreams I *(1961–1965).*

THE WORLD'S OLDEST DRAWING, FOUND IN SOUTH AFRICA

About 73,000 years ago, an early human in South Africa used a piece of ocher to scratch a mark resembling a hashtag onto a piece of stone. Archaeologists think that it may be the earliest known drawing in history. This stone was found in Blombos Cave, about 185 miles east of Cape Town, South Africa, in the early 1990s. The stone predates other early cave art found in Spain and Indonesia by approximately 30,000 years. This discovery changed the current theory of the emergence of behaviorally modern *Homo sapiens* to much earlier than previously thought.

Archaeologists also found a smooth flake of silcrete, which is a mineral formed when gravel and sand meld together. This flake contains scratchlike markings that are covered in a red pigment made from ocher. Other pieces of evidence indicating that these early *Homo sapiens* were artistic include beads, shells, and pieces of bone that had ocher on them, and some artifacts looked like they may have been a liquid form of ocher pigment at one time.

This discovery shows that drawing and painting were part of the cultural behavior of these early humans. Although researchers cannot definitively agree that these cross-hatchings are art, they do agree that the markings were probably meant to be used as a symbol, either as an abstract concept or an intentional decision to draw something artistic.

The engravings on this piece of ocher are believed to be the earliest known drawing in history.

THE MAGICAL ART OF THE MAGHREB

The Maghreb is a part of North Africa that includes Libya, Tunisia, Algeria, and Morocco. The art of the Maghreb has a mystical quality that often contains signs and symbols that originate from pre-Islamic Berber themes that were introduced in the seventh century. This art comprises a complex mixture of signs, symbols, and numbers found on painted wood and other items. Artists of the Maghreb often use secret symbols in their work that were meant as a metaphor of protest over the colonial policies that were forced upon the people.

Artists such as Gouider Triki, from Tunisia, use supernatural signs and symbols that had been found in ancient rock paintings. Other artists, such as the Kabyle women in Algeria, use their fingers to paint on the walls of their homes, creating Neolithic symbols and shapes that are meant to provide healing magic and guard against the "evil eye" and bad luck.

Some Maghreb artists rely on local materials to create their paintings, such as natural dyes and canvases made from handmade paper, wood, lambskin, and copper. The irregular shape of the lambskin helps to form the mystical background that incorporates the signs, symbols, and numbers in this art. Common symbols that are used include crescents, stars, dots, triangles, diamonds, lozenges, and odd numbers.

A Maghreb mural containing Arabic calligraphy.

The artist Ahmed Cherkaoui (1934–1967) used repetitive abstract signs and symbols with bright colors of red, blue, yellow, and green against a white background. Similar colors are used by other Maghreb artists who are self-taught. Artists such as Baya Mahieddine (1931–1998) have used highly stylized grapes and fish to honor the cycle of life of women and imaginary animals. The German artist Paul Klee was inspired by these magical shapes, symbols, and numbers and used them in his own work, which in turn inspired several Maghreb artists.

ARTFUL AFRICAN ANIMALS

Throughout time, the people of Africa have been reliant on the land and its animals for survival. Because of this, many African tribes gained an acute insight into the defining traits of the animals of the region, helping them to depict the relationship between man and nature. Art has a way of defining the individual self and one's culture, and for many African artists, animals have become a favorite subject matter. Painters often depict animals that are associated with spirits who disguise themselves in a different form.

Some African artists use symbolism and abstract concepts of animals rather than presenting realistic forms. The qualities of these animals are transported to humans or other objects to convey the animals' qualities. For example, a human may be given the head of a lion or a snake but still retains its human body. But the art does not always have to resemble an animal. An artist might choose the hair, skin, or bones of an animal to represent a particular message.

Each animal in the wild symbolizes a certain characteristic or trait. Lions are known for having courage and being regal. Elephants are associated with strength, power, and patience. Crocodiles symbolize evil spirits and have been painted on masks to chase away evil from a village. A fox represents cleverness, and a leopard represents a quick nature.

An elephant painting spotted on a wall in Zanzibar.

THE TINGATINGA SCHOOL OF PAINTING

The Mozambique-born artist E. S. Tingatinga painted for only four years, from 1968 to 1972. Although his painting life was relatively short (he died in 1972, at 40 years of age), he had a great influence on a number of young Tanzanian painters who claimed his style and developed it to become known as the Tingatinga school of painting. He is best known for painting the "big five" animals of Africa (lion, giraffe, elephant, hippopotamus, and antelope), as well as tourist-friendly landscapes such as Mount Kilimanjaro.

The Tingatinga school of painting is a concept of art that can be defined by painting on Masonite using bicycle paint in vibrant colors. Paintings can be large or small in size, but a majority of buyers are foreigners that want to transport the images out of the country, so it has come to be known as a kind of "airport art" made by younger artists. The animals featured on the paintings are typically drawn so that the whole animal fits into the frame of the Masonite, or two animals may be intertwined with each other.

Tingatinga style paintings are sold at a market in Tanzania.

CHAPTER ② ASIA

Asia has a long and colorful history of representing an eclectic balance of humankind and nature in its art. From the ancient pottery of Mesopotamia to the modern-day manga of Japan, Asian art continues to evolve and reinvent itself to express the culture and society of the Asian people.

CHINA'S LANDSCAPE PAINTING TRADITION

Chinese depictions of landscapes are much more than just pictures of mountains and the sea. They often express the longing that the artist felt for nature and a representation of Taoist principles, which seek to bring harmony between humanity and the rest of the natural world. Landscape painting is considered the most refined of Chinese painting styles.

Chinese artists were painting landscapes long before the Renaissance artists of Europe. The tradition dates back to before the Tang Dynasty (618-907 CE). There were two schools of landscape painting during this time. The first was led by Li Sixun and his son Li Zhaodao. They emphasized the use of blue and green in their works, which earned them the nickname "blue-green landscapes." The second school was led by Wang Wei, a painter and poet who painted in a spontaneous method called *pomo*. His approach enlisted a variety of shades and ink washes. These schools were known as the Northern school and the Southern school, respectively.

Landscape paintings were usually painted on silk because the artists used many layers of paint and paper was not durable enough for the job. With silk, the artist could apply hundreds of layers of paint to a landscape. The artists of this time emphasized muted washes

Jing Hao was a Chinese landscape painter. His style is known as Northern Landscape painting.

of watercolors and ink. The finished paintings were typically mounted on hanging scrolls, fans, or handscrolls.

By the Yuan Dynasty (1279–1368), the Chinese elite had retreated to their mountain homes to escape the chaos that ensued after the Mongols invaded China. They used their estates as cultural gathering places, where they discussed and created literature, painting, and poetry. Painters and calligraphers in China were traditionally well educated and highly regarded in Chinese society.

Throughout much of its history, Chinese landscape painting largely resisted outside influences—until the 1920s, that is, when artists began to incorporate the Japanese style. Many Chinese artists also integrated European art traditions into their landscapes, traveling to Germany and Paris as well as Japan to paint.

Today, the art of Chinese landscape painting retains much of the same strategy of setting the landscape scene with mountains beside a river to create a sense of space.

A Chinese landscape painter at work.

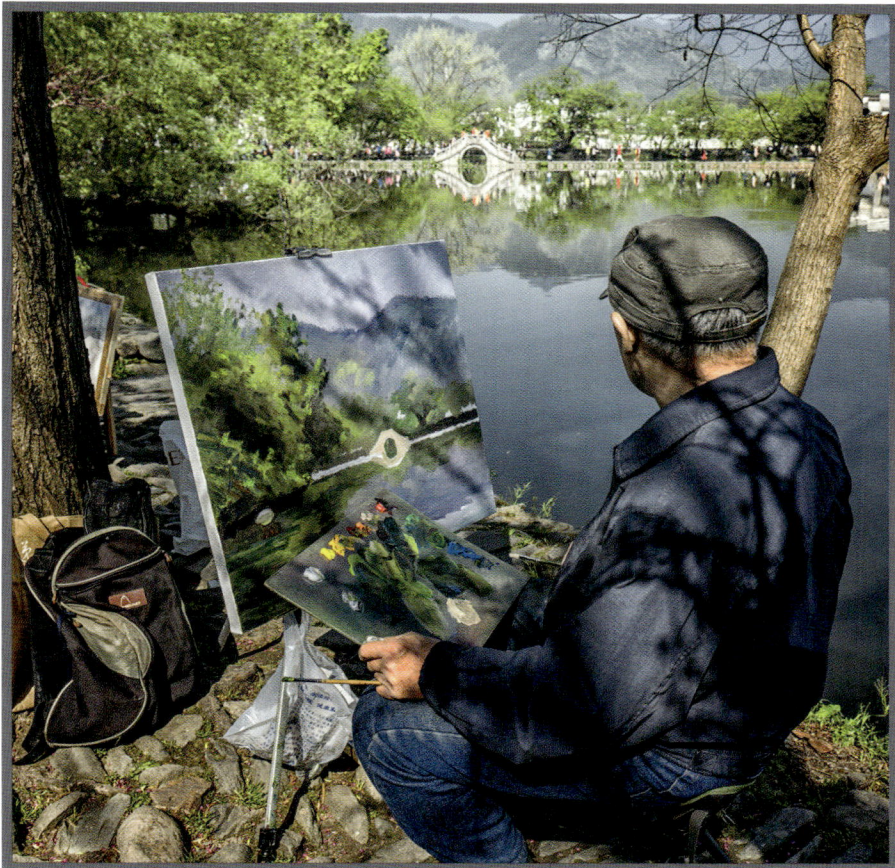

MANGA MANIA

The word *manga* comes from two Japanese words: *man*, meaning "whimsical," and ga, meaning "pictures." The first manga originated from scrolls dating from the twelfth century, but around 1800 people began using the word to describe picture books, such as *Shiji no Yukikai* by Santō Kyōden and *Manga Hyakujo* by Aikawa Minwa. Manga really took off in the 1950s. Since then, it has become so popular that manga books account for a significant share of Japan's publishing industry. In 2017 the manga market in Japan was valued at nearly $4 billion. Suffice it to say, manga is wildly popular in Japan and has a growing number of fans around the world.

Typically printed in black and white, manga books appeal to people of all ages and both genders. Their themes vary widely, from comedy, horror, action adventure, and science fiction to romance. Manga for children is designed in a simple style and tends to revolve around the theme of good conquering evil. The characters in children's manga are usually drawn with overly large eyes to easily convey emotion and are dressed in a *kawaii*, or cute, style.

Manga for teenagers and young adults tends to have a darker tone, but the

Manga is a hugely popular genre in Japan's publishing industry.

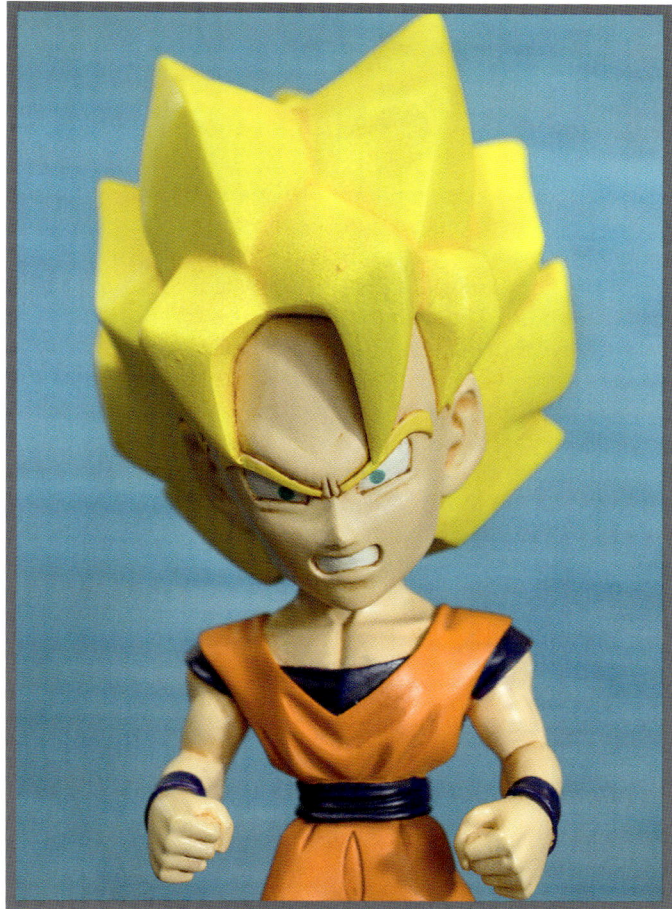

Perhaps one of the best known manga is Dragon Ball. *It has gone beyond the realms of written work with television shows, movies, bobblehead dolls, and so much more.*

premise of good triumphing over evil is still there. Although the artistic style for this age group is more detailed and realistic, it retains the stylized aesthetic with exaggerated body parts of the children's manga.

The manga comics that we know today grew out of the work of the pioneering artists of the 1950s. Manga falls into four main audience categories: boys, girls, teens, and adults. If a manga gains popularity, it is made into an anime, a Japanese-style animation. Some examples of anime include *Pokémon*, *Dragon Ball*, and *Beyblade*.

Manga has a big presence in Japanese culture. Not surprisingly, Tokyo hosts major comic book events every year. There are also manga cafés, called *manga kissa*, where customers can read the manga of their choice in a private booth for a prepaid period, which includes Internet service and nonalcoholic drinks.

GHOSTS AND MONSTERS IN JAPANESE ART

Ghosts, demons, and monsters are deeply rooted in Japanese folklore. The mythology and superstition surrounding these otherworldly creatures allowed people to rationalize their fear of death and other natural events. For the Japanese, spirits are always around us. In the Shinto religion, after a person dies, they become a spirit or a deity. These spirits inhabit the forests, the seas, the mountains, and even the air that we breathe. Some spirits are good, and some are evil.

In late nineteenth-century Kabuki theater, vengeful spirits were the main characters in many plays. Kabuki theater is a classical form of Japanese dance-drama. The performers sing and dance while wearing highly stylized makeup and costumes. One of the classic themes in Kabuki theater involves a woman who is murdered and then turns into a ghost to avenge her killers. These plays were hugely popular, and print artists would piggyback on their popularity by creating and selling drawings and paintings of scenes from the plays.

A traditional Kabuki performance. Scenes like this would often be adapted into artwork by print artists.

A depiction of Tengu by Japanese artist Kawanabe Kyōsai.

Japanese demons are in a class by themselves. They can do good or evil, have supernatural powers, and can affect the forces of nature. The Oni, for example, are creatures depicted with horns and tiger skins. They have big mouths and clawed fingers, dress in red, and have big hair and no neck. They represent the evil parts of human nature and are responsible for disease and sickness. The Tengu, in contrast, are mountain demons who live in forests. Artists depict these creatures in a couple of ways: with beards and big lumpy noses, or as humans with a bird's head and clawed feet with wings spread apart. The Tengu can transform themselves into little people and trick humans with nasty pranks.

Some animals were believed to have had supernatural powers, too. The raccoon and the fox were two of the most popular animals. Artists pictured these animals as mischievous and often getting themselves into trouble. A fox, called a *kitsune*, could change its shape, but its face would remain that of a fox. In some stories, they often pretended to be humans to trick men into making unwise decisions.

Many Japanese legends feature dragons and snakes with magical powers. Traditionally, artists drew stylized dragons with horns, wide mouths, and long fangs. Dragons in art represent the forces of nature, such as floods or other natural disasters. There are four types of dragons: heavenly dragons that guard the gods, earth dragons that take care of the rivers, spiritual dragons that bring rain, and dragons that guard earthly treasures.

THE FINE ART OF CHINESE CALLIGRAPHY

Throughout Chinese history, calligraphy has been considered a supreme visual art form. Calligraphy, which means "beautiful writing," seeks its inspiration from the forces of nature. Early examples of calligraphy can be found on the bones of animals and turtle shells from around 1600 to 1100 BCE. The Shang kings used these objects in rituals to help them divine the future.

Calligraphers use brushes, ink, paper, and inkstone to create this individualized art form. Calligraphy brushes come in various shapes and sizes and are made of different kinds of animal hair, such as rabbit, goat, or weasel. The ink is made from a sooty powder created from pine resin called "lampblack." It is mixed with glue and then molded into a cakelike shape that is often etched with a decorative pattern. Paper can be made from fibers, such as bamboo, hemp, mulberry, or silk.

The most talented calligraphers must use a combination of imagination and skill to coax each character into unique shapes and strokes without any retouching or reshading. It takes years of practice to achieve this balance of skill and self-expression.

A Chinese calligrapher master using his brush and ink.

PREHISTORIC ASIAN ART AND THE ART OF MESOPOTAMIA

Mesopotamia was settled by hunter-gatherer peoples around 10,000 BCE and is referred to as the "cradle of civilization." This area occupied what is now Northeastern Syria, Southeastern Turkey, Southwestern Iran, and Iraq.

The Sumerians (around 5000 BCE) were artisans and craftsmen who worked in gold, copper, and lapis, as well as wood and clay. They made musical instruments and chairs, but their most exceptional work was their painted pottery, which was so highly valued that they used it as a kind of money. The Sumerians traded pottery for items such as food and clothes. The pottery was decorated with geometric designs or pictures of people and animals, such as bulls or lions.

Later, the Babylonians also worked with lapis, gold, clay, and wood, and they created pieces similar to those of the Sumerians, such as musical instruments, statues, mosaics, and pottery. The Assyrians lived to the north of the Babylonians and conquered Babylon in 934 CE. They created murals and paintings that usually depicted people hunting or fighting. They also painted murals that showed how Assyrian royalty lived.

A piece of pottery from the ancient Assyrians.

THE *MEHNDI* ART OF INDIA

Mehndi has been used as a cosmetic in India for at least 5,000 years. Otherwise known as "henna tattoos," *mehndi* uses a red-orange ink made from the henna plant to decorate the hands, feet, and other parts of the body. Different shades of color can be created by mixing other kinds of leaves, such as tea, cloves, lemon, and tamarind, with the henna. *Mehndi* is used by women and children for celebrations, such as weddings, holidays, and other special occasions.

After the henna leaves are dried, they are ground into a powder and mixed with hot water to make a paste. The paste is then applied over a pattern on the skin and left to dry overnight. After the paste is removed, the decorated area on the skin will continue to darken for around three days, and the images can last for a month or more.

During weddings, the bride and groom, along with other members of the wedding party, are decorated with *mehndi* to signify a *barakah*, or blessing, which is considered good luck. Sometimes the name of the bride and groom will be hidden in the *mehndi* design, and the groom must try and find it. The most talented *mehndi* artists command high fees for their work.

A bride is decorated with mehndi *before her wedding.*

FOLDING SCREENS OF JAPAN

Japanese folding screens are called *byōbu*. They are composed of long, rectangular panels with silk borders that often have artwork and calligraphy painted on them. They originally came to Japan from Korea in 686 CE. The first folding screens were very heavy and awkward to use, because the panels were hinged with leather cords or silk. In the fourteenth century CE, folding screens used hinges made of a paper called *kami chotsugi*. These hinges connected the panels in a sturdy fashion that allowed the artwork on the screen to be seen while standing upright in a zigzag pattern. Many of the scenes on *byōbu* are of landscapes and peaceful views of nature.

Byōbu are used to divide a room and create a private or intimate area. These folding screens were often decorated with gold foil and placed behind a statue or icon of a religious image. When people were finished using them, the screens were easy to fold away and store until they were needed again. The style of the *byōbu* has evolved over time and reflects the diversity and culture of the different regions of Japan. Styles and themes vary widely, from simple, monochromatic designs to rich and highly detailed landscapes decorated with gold.

A Japanese folding screen.

BUDDHIST MURALS OF THAILAND

Buddhist murals in Thailand began as an attempt by the monks to teach common folk about the teachings of Buddha. The east and west walls inside a temple would each display a particular theme.

- The west wall was associated with death and showed scenes painted with ghosts and otherworldly beings.
- The east wall had views depicting the Buddha subduing the demon Mara, surrounded by more benign demons, with celestial beings above him.

Other murals in Buddhist temples showed representations of the Buddha in his former lives and sometimes humorous and bawdy scenes of the villagers while at work or play. Because walls of temples were easily damaged by weather, few of the older murals have survived.

A Buddhist mural inside a temple.

THE JOSEON DYNASTY OF KOREAN PAINTING

Yi Seong-gye, a military commander who founded the Joseon Dynasty (1392–1894), wanted to reform Korean society. He partnered with like-minded Confucian scholars to reorganize Korean life according to Confucian principles and teachings. These teachings were based on a belief in peace, order, proper manners, and a desire to strengthen harmonious relationships among all people.

In the later part of the Joseon Dynasty, artists primarily painted for their patrons, who were called the Yangban, a privileged and educated class of men who dominated government and military positions. The Yangban had a taste for artwork that was restrained and simple. Many examples of artwork from this period portray government officials, ancestors, landscapes, and simple scenes of everyday life. By the mid-1700s, many artists began to be influenced by the Western approach to space and form. In contrast, the folk painting of the Joseon Dynasty was much more lighthearted. Artists used bold colors and humorous themes that were geared toward selling to the less-educated classes.

A Boat Ride by Joseon Dynasty artist Shin Yun-bok.

VIETNAMESE SILK PAINTING

The art of Vietnamese silk painting originated from drawing and painting on home-made rice paper. Although artists have been making silk paintings since the fifteenth century, this artistic style reached its popularity between 1925 and 1945. Vietnamese silk painting is known for its use of bright colors and simple themes, with an emphasis on elegance and softness. These silk paintings can include a wide range of themes, including landscapes, scenes of everyday life, such as a farmer with his oxen, or a young girl reading by a calm and peaceful lake.

   The background of the painting starts on a canvas of silk that is starched and woven. The background is not painted but uses the color of the silk itself. Many artists of Vietnamese silk paintings are known by the color of the canvas that they use, and they carefully consider the quality and color of the silk before starting a painting. Artists generally use watercolors for this style of silk painting, and they must be very precise in their brushstrokes because they cannot erase mistakes. After a work is finished, it is placed in a bamboo scroll frame.

A Vietnamese silk painting on display.

CHAPTER ❸ EUROPE

From the angelic Renaissance paintings of Botticelli and Michelangelo to the explosive and expanding movement of Lisbon graffiti and street art, Europe has something for all tastes in artistic style. Come along on this art adventure to discover the rich history and culture of European art.

ITALIAN RENAISSANCE ART

Following the Middle Ages, the Italian Renaissance lasted from the beginning of the fourteenth century to the early sixteenth century. During this period, there was a revival of interest in the ideas and values of ancient Greece and Rome. This art movement sought to express the experiences of the individual and the beauties of the natural world.

Because of a newfound political stability and general prosperity, new technologies were developed during the Italian Renaissance, including the printing press. There were also enormous advances in the technical aspects of painting that helped artists depict the human body much more realistically.

The Catholic Church was a major patron of artists, as were civil governments and wealthy merchant families, such as the Medici family in Florence. Many of the paintings created during the Renaissance included religious subjects, focusing on people like the Virgin Mary. Many of these pieces were used as devotional objects or altarpieces that were incorporated into rituals of the Catholic Mass.

During the High Renaissance (1490s–1527), artists like Michelangelo, Raphael, and Leonardo da Vinci became experts at using new approaches to painting subjects that included portraying their themes with the use of light and shadow

Michelangelo's paintings inside the Medici Chapel in Florence, Italy.

and at depicting the relationships between animals, humans, and their surrounding landscapes. Renaissance artists came from all walks of life and typically studied as apprentices to a master before they were allowed to be admitted into a professional guild. Artists in a guild usually worked on commission and were hired by patrons from the middle and wealthy classes to paint sacred images, portraits, and domestic themes such as a birth, marriage, or everyday family life.

In the fifteenth and sixteenth centuries, artists such as Titian and Giorgione developed an artistic method of painting directly on the canvas with oil paints. This kind of technique enabled the artist to rework his image as he pleased, unlike fresco painting, which required painting directly on plaster and left little room for changes.

By the end of the fifteenth century, many cities in Italy, including Milan, Mantua, Venice, and Bologna, were considered great artistic centers. Each city had its own distinct characteristics in painting styles. For example, the artists of Milan preferred to emphasize the visual effects of perspective, whereas artists in Bologna wanted to follow the traditions of Raphael and other central Italian artists who were trying to create paintings that were suggestive of poetry.

Wealthy patrons like the Borgia and Medici families commissioned many famous masterpieces, such as *Birth of Venus* by Sandro Botticelli and *The Last Supper* by Leonardo da Vinci. The works that these wealthy and influential families commissioned were meant to convey a message regarding their power and authority. Artists were also hired to paint portraits of women. Although the laws of the time prohibited the use of extravagant dress, female subjects of portraits wore their finest clothes, with elaborate jewels and intricate hairpieces to indicate their status. Parents commissioned portraits of their daughters to show off their family's wealth, and they were often shown to prospective husbands to help secure an engagement or wedding proposal.

Leonardo da Vinci's **The Last Supper**.

THE CHEEKY ART OF BANKSY AND THE STREET ART MOVEMENT

When the British graffiti master Banksy was selected by *Time* magazine as one of the world's 100 most influential people in 2010, he gave the editors a picture of himself with a recyclable paper bag over his head. Banksy is notoriously private with his identity, and his fans prefer it that way. He has not had a face-to-face interview since 2003.

After nearly being caught by the police for spraying graffiti on a train, Banksy came up with the idea of using stencils to save time on his painting projects. He started out as a graffiti artist "bombing" the walls in Bristol, England, in the 1990s, but he now can command hundreds of thousands of dollars or more for his artwork at the biggest auction houses in Britain.

Banksy's first exhibition took place in 2001. He and several other artists set up decorator's signs in the alley on Rivington Street, painted the walls of the alleyway white, and then hung their artwork. About 500 people showed up, and it cost them almost nothing to set up the show. In 2003 Banksy had his breakthrough exhibition, titled Turf War, which was staged with a carnival-like atmosphere and

Banksy's Naked Man *appears on the side of a building in Bristol, England.*

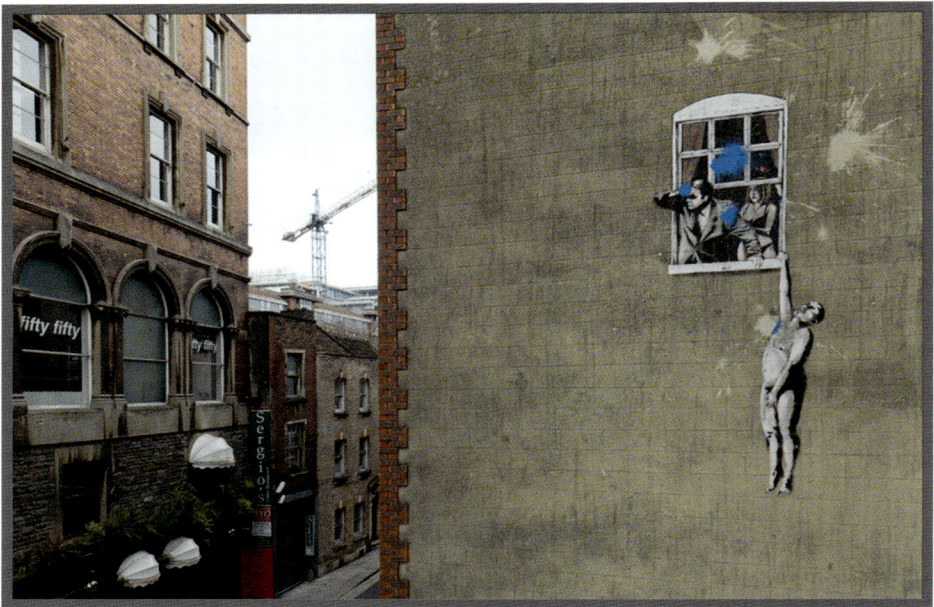

featured a live cow painted with a portrait of Andy Warhol and a chimpanzee dressed as Queen Elizabeth II.

Banksy's most common form of street art is still stenciling. He uses a multilayered format of stencils in combination with spray paint and other media, such as found objects or street signs. His work is often cheeky and satirical and contains elements of philosophy and politics.

Like Banksy, among the hidden alleys, abandoned buildings, and subway tunnels of Europe are other street artists looking to make their mark. They paint the walls to put their soul on display, and there are several cities in Europe where you can see their artwork. When the Berlin Wall came down, many artists saw an opportunity to try to beautify the drab and dank Communist side of the city. Berlin now contains one of the biggest concentrations of street art. The so-called East Side Gallery, located on a remnant of the east side of the Berlin Wall, features over 100 works by various artists.

In the 1990s, Barcelona, Spain, was one of the first European cities to welcome the work of graffiti and street artists. After the passage of restrictive laws discouraging street art in 2006, "free walls" began to spring up where artists could express themselves without recrimination. Lisbon is an especially good place to view street art because of an official effort to cooperate with and support artists. In 2010 the Crono Project was formed to encourage street artists to beautify derelict buildings with their paintings.

Paris is known for the Louvre, but it has also been the home to many street artists since the 1960s. Street artists such as Invader, Jef Aerosol, and Blek le Rat have all made their mark on the city of Paris. Thus, no matter where you go in Europe, you are bound to view some street art. From explosions of bright colors to political statements to the cheeky art of Banksy, street art uses the world as a canvas, and it is having a renaissance of its own that just keeps on growing.

The Berlin Wall is filled with street art from multiple artists.

WOMEN PAINTERS OF EUROPE

Women artists have been involved in creating what can be considered fine art throughout history, but they have often been overlooked in favor of their male counterparts. Women have been faced with gender biases that tend to consider them being good at only "arts and crafts" or fiber arts. But beginning in the late 1960s, women artists created a feminist art movement that sought to address their role in the art world and to feature the artwork of women of the past, present, and future, and of all races and ethnicities.

Starting in the late eighteenth century, French women painters began to gain professional success, and they were some of the most sought-after artists in Paris by 1780. This success came despite women being barred from life-drawing classes and an acceptance limit on women attending the art school at Académie Royale de Peinture et de Sculpture.

The most important patrons for many women artists during the eighteenth century were royal women. Artists such as Anne Vallayer-Coster (1744–1818) were hired to paint scenes of everyday family life and portraits, but she was best known for her still lifes of flowers with fruits and seashells. She eventually won the patronage of Queen Marie Antoinette and Mesdames Adélaide and Victoire, the daughters of King Louis XV.

The beginning of the French Revolution made it much more difficult for French women artists to continue their careers, mainly because of their associations with the royal family, and many artists, including Vallayer-Coster, fled the country to find patrons at other courts in England, Russia, and elsewhere in Europe.

In Italy, women artists learned their skill from their fathers, such

Anne Vallayer-Coster's portrait of Queen Marie Antoinette.

Fede Galizia's Portrait of Paolo Morigia.

as Fede Galizia (1578–1630), who became an accomplished artist by the age of 12. She was the daughter of Nunzio Galizia, a portrait painter who taught her to draw and paint. Fede was known for her skill as a portrait artist, and she excelled at painting clothing and jewelry. She was also commissioned for religious paintings and still lifes. Indeed, her technique in painting still lifes was considered pioneering and was emulated by other artists.

More recently, Paula Rego, who was born in 1935, was a member of the artist collective the "London Group," which included Frank Auerbach, David Hockney, and R. B. Kitaj. Rego's work incorporates themes that relate to the folklore of her native Portugal. Over the course of her career, her style has changed from abstract to representational, and it contains colorful and intricate designs that include elements of political consciousness.

THE MASTER OF SHOCK: FRANCISCO GOYA

Francisco José de Goya y Lucientes (1746–1828) holds an interesting position in the history of Western art because he can be considered both an Old Master and a modern artist. Over the span of his career, his painting style ranged from lighthearted elements of Romanticism sprinkled with imagination and emotion to dark and pessimistic statements regarding the sometimes chaotic events of his day, such as the interrogations of the Inquisition and the aftermath of the Napoleonic Wars.

At age 14, Goya began studying with a painter named José Luzán y Martínez (1710–1785). He failed at two attempts in drawing competitions for the Real Academia des Bellas Artes but began working for the royal workshops in 1774. This position lasted for the rest of his life. He started out by doing preliminary paintings, or tapestry cartoons, for the Royal Tapestry Factory in Santa Bárbara, which depicted leisurely activities in a Rococo style. During this time, Goya created *The Blind Guitarist*, but it was rejected by the factory weavers because the design was too complex.

Goya also received many commissions for portraits and family paintings from the aristocracy, such as the *Condesa de Altamira and Her Daughter*, which high-light his painterly skills and his use of broad brushstrokes and play of light. When he turned 40 years old, he was appointed the painter to King Charles III, and then promoted to court painter to Charles IV in 1789. But France declared war with Spain in 1793, and Goya began traveling to other parts of Spain. He fell ill while in Cádiz and ended up totally deaf, but he was able to return to his position as court painter.

By 1799 Goya's paintings and etchings took a much darker turn, with works such as *Out Hunting for Teeth* and *The Sleep of Reason Produces Monsters*. These works introduced a whole world of fantastic, nightmarish witches and ghosts that were meant to symbolize his version of the world against reason.

In 1808 Napoleon's armies invaded Spain and executed Spanish citizens who voiced their opposition. Napoleon's brother, Joseph, assumed leadership of Spain, and Goya was forced to pledge allegiance to the regime. He ended up painting members of the French regime and was awarded the Royal Order of Spain in 1811.

By 1814 the French had restored the Spanish Republic. But Ferdinand VII, the new king, was power hungry. He revoked the constitution and declared himself absolute monarch. Goya's loyalty to the new government was ques-tioned, and he responded by painting *The Second of May 1808*, a brutal scene depicting Spaniards fighting the French on horseback. The painting embellishes dark tones and fluid brushstrokes influenced by artists such as Rembrandt and Velázquez.

Goya's The Second of May.

Goya received no painting commissions from Ferdinand VII, and he began to isolate himself from social and political life. He retired to his country house, Quinta del Sordo (the Deaf Man's House), and began a series of paintings known as the Black Paintings. They are unnerving and sinister in theme, featuring horrifying scenes with dark tones.

MARC CHAGALL AND THE RUSSIAN MODERNISTS

Marc Chagall was born in Russia in 1887. He valued his Jewish identity and incorporated many elements of Jewish culture into his artworks. His figurative and narrative style also borrowed components from Fauvism, Surrealism, and Cubism. In 1910 Chagall moved to France and became a member of the École de Paris. By the 1920s, the emerging Surrealist movement had claimed Chagall as one of its own, but he ultimately rejected this approach, even though much of his work contains a dreamlike and supernatural quality.

One of Chagall's early works, an oil on canvas titled *I and the Village* (1911), depicts a playful interpretation of the Russian countryside with both Fauvist and Cubist influences. It is painted in an abstract, figurative, and modern style, with a cow who dreams of a milk maid while a man and wife play in the work fields. In 1913 Chagall painted *Paris through the Window*. In this work, Chagall searches for beauty in the details, with a depiction of a figure in the bottom right looking both ways, a couple that seems to be splitting apart underneath the Eiffel Tower, and a cat looking out a window from a building above. This painting has a supernatural quality, and the end result is a brilliant visual balance of a Paris scene that mixes the real and the imaginary.

The viewer sees a more somber side of Chagall in *Bella with White Collar* (1917). This painting is a portrait of Chagall's first wife, Bella, whom he married in 1915. Her face is pointed downward, and she stands over a lush country landscape. Below Bella are two smaller figures who represent Chagall and the couple's daughter, Ida. Although Chagall used the same vibrant colors in this work, it is clear that he was a master of painting traditional subjects in addition to more abstract themes.

Chagall's Bella with White Collar.

THE UNCONSCIOUS WORLD OF SURREALISM

Surrealism is part of an art movement that began in the 1920s. It allowed artists to express themselves through their subconscious and aimed at creating a painted world in which the conditions of dreams and reality melded into a kind of super-reality.

Surrealism developed after the Dada movement following World War I and was centered in Paris, France. The leader of Surrealism was André Breton, a poet and critic, who believed that Surrealism was a revolutionary movement focused on positive expression and a reaction to the destruction that was caused by the "rationalism" that preceded the events leading up to World War I. Breton explained that Surrealism was a way of reuniting the conscious and subconscious world to tap into one's imagination. Surrealist painting was influenced by Dadaism and inspired by the fantastical and often bizarre images of artists such as Francisco Goya, Hieronymus Bosch, and Marc Chagall.

Some of the major Surrealist artists were Salvador Dalí, Joan Miró, René Magritte, Max Ernst, and Jean Arp. Each of these artists found their own way to interpret their idea of Surrealism and took it as a starting point to free their sub-conscious mind to explore personal fantasies. Generally, the themes of Surrealism often investigated fully recognizable scenes that were interspersed with elements that were paradoxical or shocking to evoke a response in the viewer. For example, in Magritte's painting *The Portrait,* a seemingly simple still life of a table setting with a slice of ham on a plate and a bottle of wine is transformed into a surreal image by adding a human eye into the center of the ham.

A museumgoer observes Salvador Dalí's Soft Construction with Boiled Beans (Premonition of Civil War).

THE CELTIC ART OF IRELAND

Celtic art originated with people known as the Celts, and this form of art covers a huge expanse of time, perhaps beginning in the Neolithic Age. However, art historians generally refer to Celtic art as that created from about the fifth century BCE onward. Celtic art style is primarily ornamental and favors the use of geometrical decoration that is extremely stylized and often symbolic. Such decorations may contain circular patterns, spirals, zoomorphics, interlocking loops, plant forms, and key patterns. Spirals, one of the oldest symbols used in Celtic art, symbolize the life force.

Over time, Celtic art merged with other influences, such as Christianity. For example, the *Book of Kells* is an illuminated manuscript thought to have been created by the Irish sometime around 800 CE. It contains the four gospels from the New Testament and is heavily decorated with Celtic artwork.

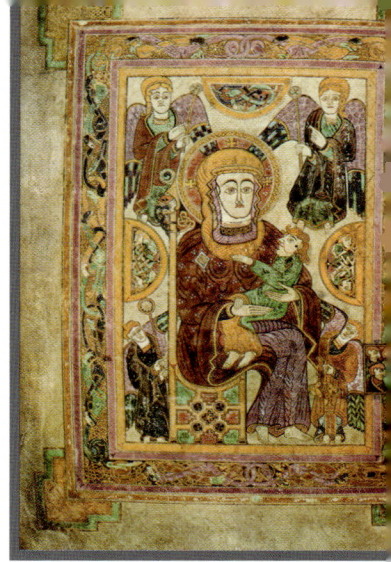
This artwork from the Book of Kells *depicts the Virgin Mary and her child.*

GREEK MURALS

During the Hellenistic period, the Greeks highly valued the arts, and learning how to paint was a staple of a good education. Many paintings were created on wood panels or in fresco in a Mycenaean style, although very little samples have survived from this time period.

Ancient Greece spawned several traditions of painting. Early forms were similar to the process of painting vases, with a strong emphasis placed on the drawing's outline and painting flat areas of color. But by the end of the Hellenistic period, techniques advanced to include contours in form and shadows, some foreshortening, and the use of changing colors to indicate distance in the background of a landscape. The most common form of art was panel painting—usually painted on wooden boards with tempura and encaustic wax. These paintings usually depicted scenes of figures, portraits, and still lifes.

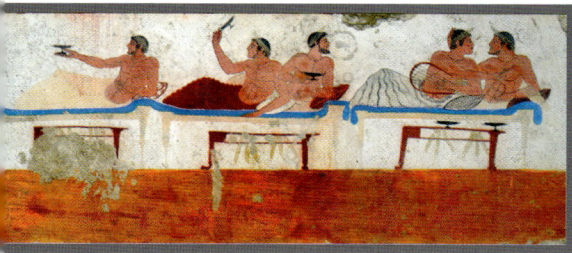
An ancient Greek fresco found on the wall of a tomb.

ART MASTERPIECES OF VATICAN CITY

Vatican City is home to one of the world's greatest art collections, with works by artists such as Raphael, Titian, Michelangelo, and Leonardo da Vinci. The ceiling of the Sistine Chapel was painted by Michelangelo between 1508 and 1512 and is an example of High Renaissance art.

Michelangelo's painting of *The Last Judgment,* which covers the altar wall of the Sistine Chapel, encompasses around 390 people surrounding the Christ figure, almost all of whom are nude. It represents the resurrection of the dead at the second coming of Christ. The people depicted in the painting are separated into those who will be saved and those who will be damned. Shortly after Michelangelo died, people objected to the nude figures and other artists were hired to cover them with fig leaves and branches. However, the figures were restored to their original form during the chapel's restoration, which began in 1979.

One of the most famous paintings in Vatican City is in the Raphael Rooms; it is called the *School of Athens* by Raphael. This painting represents a gathering of scholars and artists from the scholarly worlds of philosophy and science.

Raphael's School of Athens.

FRENCH IMPRESSIONISM

The art movement known as Impressionism started in France in the mid-nineteenth century and was inspired by anti-establishment sentiment and a desire to paint aspects of modern life rather than subjects such as history or mythology. One early example of Impressionism from 1872 was Claude Monet's landscape titled *Impression, Sunrise*.

During this time, Paris had only one state-sponsored place to exhibit artwork and develop a reputation as an artist. Artists who were not chosen by the jury for the exhibition would have to wait a whole year to apply again. So Monet and his friends, including Edgar Degas, August Renoir, Alfred Sisley, and Berthe Morisot, among others, decided to put on their own exhibition. They pooled their money, rented a studio, and set a date for the show. Monet and his artist friends decided to call themselves the Anonymous Society of Painters, Sculptors, and Printmakers. This first exhibition opened on April 15, 1874, and they held eight more exhibitions from 1874 to 1886.

Initially, critics felt that the artwork from these exhibitions was terrible and lacked the finish of more traditional Romantic and Neoclassical paintings. Critics labeled these artworks as merely "impressions," and said they were too sketchy and unfinished to be considered seriously. But the "Impressionist" label stuck, and they became celebrated artists.

One of the Impressionists' main intentions was to capture a particular moment in time by using certain atmospheric conditions, such as color and light. They painted *en plein air*, or outside, to capture the quickly shifting light. For example, a painting might contain moving clouds, flickering light on the water, or a sudden rain shower. They painted these scenes by painting small bits of pure color next to each other, so that when viewed at a distance, the viewer's eyes would translate the myriad bits of color into one optically blended, vibrant scene.

Claude Monet's The Bride over the Water Lily Pond.

CHAPTER 4 LATIN AMERICA AND THE CARIBBEAN

Latin America and the Caribbean have an eclectic mix of cultures that contribute to the painting and drawing of each of these areas. From the artwork of the indigenous peoples of the region to the paintings of colonialization to the art movements of political protest, artists of Latin America and the Caribbean continue to evolve and grow as they paint and draw.

THE BRAVE AND BOLD FRIDA KAHLO

Frida Kahlo was born in Mexico in 1907 and is considered one of Mexico's greatest artists. She contracted polio as a child, which caused one leg to be shorter than the other. As a teenager, she was impaled by a steel handrail in a bus accident and broke her foot, dislocated her shoulder, and suffered multiple fractures of her spine, ribs, and collarbone. Kahlo had to wear a full body cast for over three months, and she had over 30 operations during her lifetime. She turned to painting

Frida Kahlo's earliest self-portrait.

as a way to ease her pain and loneliness. She often painted while lying down in her bed because of the pain from her injuries.

Self-portraits and life experience are a common theme in Kahlo's work, which encompasses about 200 paintings, drawings, and sketches. Kahlo's earliest self-portrait is titled *Self-Portrait in a Velvet Dress*, completed in 1926. She sent it to her lover, Alejandro, in the hopes that he would renew their love affair.

Frida Kahlo was married twice to the Mexican muralist and painter Diego Rivera, whom she met when they both attended school at the National Preparatory School in Mexico City. The two began a romance after Kahlo asked him to evaluate her work in 1928. They had a tumultuous relationship, and both had numerous affairs.

By 1932 Frida Kahlo was adding more Surrealistic aspects to her painting style. During this period, she painted *Henry Ford Hospital* (1932), which depicts Kahlo lying naked in a hospital bed surrounded by floating objects such as a fetus, a snail, and a flower, all connected by veins. This painting was an expression of her sadness over having her second miscarriage. In the painting *Self-Portrait with Cropped Hair* (1940), Kahlo painted herself in a man's suit while holding a pair of scissors, with her hair all over the floor. This was meant to represent the time that she cut her hair after Rivera cheated on her.

Although she occasionally painted portraits for friends, Kahlo did not sell many paintings during her lifetime. She participated in a group exhibition in 1940, the International Exhibition of Surrealism, where she showed two of her paintings, *The Wounded Table* and *The Two Fridas*. She had one solo exhibition in 1943, just a year before her death. In 2006 her painting *Roots* sold for $5.62 million at a Sotheby's auction in New York City. This sale made Frida Kahlo one of the highest-selling women painters in history.

Frida Kahlo's **The Bus.**

THE EXPLOSION OF STREET ART IN MEXICO CITY

A large mural overlooks a Mexican market.

Mexican street art has exploded in the twenty-first century. However, culturally, Mexico has been no stranger to graffiti and murals—the Aztecs and Mayans covered their temple walls with painted images during the precolonial era. In addition, Muralism, made famous by artists such as Diego Rivera, David Siqueiros, and Jose Orozco, became a prevalent art movement after the Mexican Revolution. It seems that Mexican artists have been covering the city walls with beautiful art ever since.

Initially, modern Mexican murals focused on political themes related to politics and nationalism as a kind of propaganda to get the message out to a mostly illiterate population. But over time, Mexican artists began to express their individual voices with their own ideas and values, covering a wide range of themes that extended beyond the old ideals of politics and religion.

Many Mexican street artists consider their art a form of liberation, because it can be enjoyed by everyone regardless of class or education. This allows Mexican artists incredible exposure on a much larger stage. Street art is generally approved by the authorities, as long as the artist gets permission from the building owner.

Mexican street artists gain recognition by posting their paintings on social media sites such as Instagram, and many artists have huge followings. Mexico's street art themes continue to feature Aztec and Mayan themes, whereas others feature ideas on political and social activism. Still others are just plain quirky or cute, with bright colors and imaginary characters. Part of the fun of seeing Mexican street art is the hunt itself—traveling throughout the city in search your favorite murals, or stumbling upon one by accident that catches your imagination.

One of the best places to search for art is in the Centro neighborhood of Mexico City, which includes the Centro Histórico district. Many murals are located just outside of cafés and bars to attract guests. Other street artists paint themes according to what kind of store it is, such as a painting of a woman wearing cosmetics on the shutters of a cosmetic shop. Some murals take up the entire wall of a large building.

One interesting location that seemingly represents a museumlike atmosphere of street art is at the El Museo del Juguete Antiguo México (MUJAM), or the Antique Toy Museum of Mexico. This museum features displays of various vintage toys that are spread out over many floors. On the museum roof, you can view a gallery of sorts that features several large murals from prominent street artists.

Two artists paint a mural in Mexico City.

INDIGENOUS ART AND BODY PAINTING OF BRAZIL

The earliest cave paintings in Brazil, which can be dated back to 13,000 BCE, are located in the Serra da Capivara National Park. Before the Europeans arrived in Brazil, native people lived in tribes along the riverbed, in jungles, and on the coast. These indigenous people were probably nomadic and traveled when they needed a new food source or shelter. However, they could do little to store and preserve their art as they moved from place to place. Thus, other than cave paintings, little evidence of their art has remained.

Many tribes today use body painting as a form of art and as a way of distinguishing different social groups. The paint is a kind of ink made from vegetable and mineral dyes, such as limestone for white color, annatto for red, and genipap for dark blue. A carbon powder is then used over the paint with a layer of resin. Many of the body painting designs are geometric, with varying complex and beautiful embellishments chosen by the wearer.

The people of the Kayapó culture use body and face paint to decorate themselves for ceremonial occasions. Social insects such as bees and ants hold great significance for them. The Kayapó believe that their

The cave paintings in Brazil's Serra da Capivara National Park can be dated back to 13,000 BCE.

ancestors learned how to get along with each other as a society from these kinds of communal insects. They deeply respect and care for the environment and its animal inhabitants. When the Kayapó people dress for ceremonies, they try to reflect and respect the environment around them by using body paint, decorating themselves with the patterns of insects such as bees, spiders, beetles, ladybugs, or grasshoppers.

For the Karajá people in the Amazon region, body painting and decorative ornamentation are looked on as not only an aesthetic custom but a moral sense of obligation as well. They believe that the body is not considered human until it is transformed from a "raw," unsocial person into a "real" person.

Finally, the Panará people have a fascination with using the designs of other indigenous groups and cultures in their body painting. The Panará sometimes borrow the body paint designs of the Kayapó people, incorporating their designs and mixing them with those of the Panará. These designs

A woman from the Kayapó tribe has painted her body for the National Indian Festival.

are largely geometric, some with zigzags or straight vertical stripes. The women often have a close relative paint the designs for them, or they paint their own bodies. They apply the paint by using their hands, or they use a brush made from corn husks or palm fronds.

MASTER OF MURALS: DIEGO RIVERA

Diego Rivera and his twin brother were born in Guanajuato, Mexico, in 1885. He showed artistic talent from a young age and was enrolled at the San Carlos Academy of Fine Arts when he was 12 years old. He met fellow artist Gerardo Murillo at the Academy, and they later became the primary force in the Mexican mural movement.

After school, Rivera received a sponsorship to study in Europe, where he painted works such as *Head of a Breton Woman* and *Night Scene in Avila*. After he discovered Cubism, Rivera's painting style grew to be more abstract. Many of Rivera's themes in paintings feature stories of the working class with miners, farmers, and peasants. Rivera is best known for his mural work, such as *The Liberated Earth with Natural Forces Controlled by Man*, which was painted for the National School of Agriculture in Mexico. He was an active painter for over 50 years, from around 1907 to 1957. Rivera was politically active, considered himself a Marxist, and joined the Communist Party in 1922.

World-famous Mexican artist Diego Rivera painted large-scale murals, such as this one depicting auto workers at the Detroit Institute of Arts.

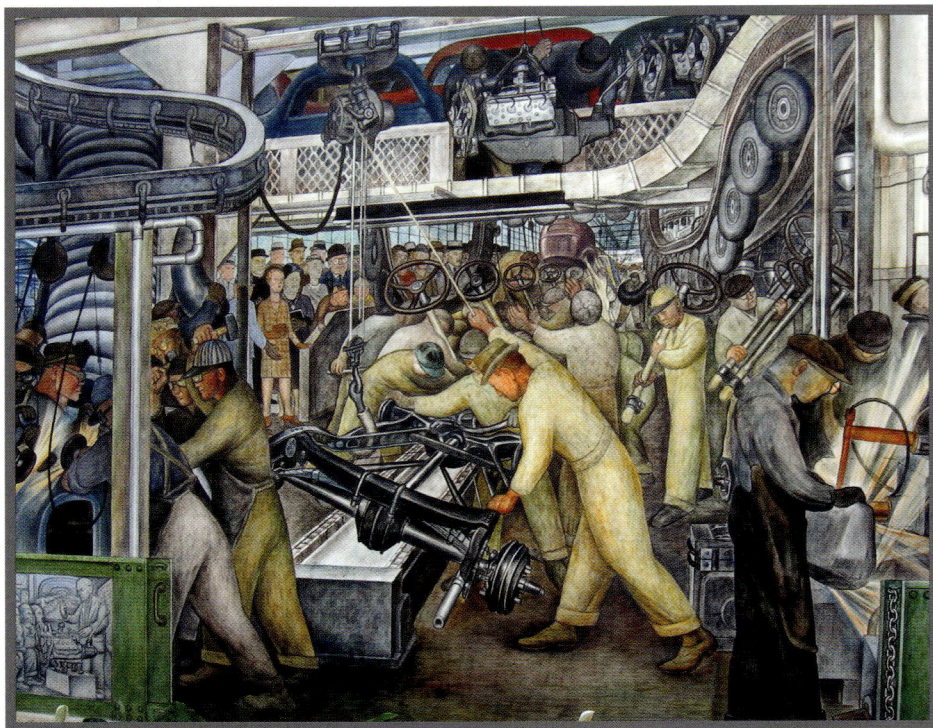

THE STUNNING AND VIBRANT COLORS OF JAMAICAN ART

The art movements of Jamaica have been heavily influenced by other art movements of Europe and America, as well as the cultural influences of the African diaspora.

Frequently referred to as the "mother of Jamaican art," Edna Manley arrived in Jamaica in 1922. She called the art scene at the time "anemic" because of its focus on European-styled landscapes and portraits, and she felt that the artworks being produced did not reflect the Jamaican culture or its people. Subsequently, Jamaican artists and thinkers of the time began to appreciate a greater sense of cultural expression that coincided with Marcus Garvey's protest movement to mobilize blacks in a "pan-African unity" and boost themselves politically and economically as a way to gain independence from oppression.

Out of these two efforts came the start of Saturday morning art classes offered at the Institute of Jamaica, and later at the Jamaica School of Art (1950), where young students were encouraged to paint subjects more closely related to Jamaican culture and everyday life. These art classes were the beginning of the Jamaican Modernist art movement, and they helped provide a means for Jamaican artists to study beyond the confines of the island, in Europe and America.

Paintings by Jamaica folk artists feature everyday life.

Since the 1960s, Jamaican art has evolved into groups with different influences. One group, known as the "intuitive" artists, has less formal training and attempts to identify with a more cultural outlook from a strictly Jamaican perspective. Ras Daniel Heartman is known for his work with the Rastafarian art movement. He created pencil and charcoal drawings of the Rasta consciousness.

Another group, referred to as the "mainstream" artists, are generally trained and are influenced by styles from Europe and other countries. The artist Barrington Watson is known as "Jamaica's master painter"; he was educated at the Royal College of Art in London and the Académie de la Grande Chaumiére in Paris. Barrington's Realist style explores many different themes, such as landscapes, still lifes, nudes, and self-portraits.

MODERN AND CONTEMPORARY ART OF CUBA

Since the easing of travel and economic restrictions were implemented by President Barak Obama in 2014, art collectors have begun to look more seriously at artists and their work in Cuba. Contemporary artists in Cuba continue to gain recognition as more and more interest in Cuban culture grows.

One such artist is Alicia Leal, who graduated from the oldest art school in Cuba, the San Alejandro School of Fine Arts, and started to be noticed in the 1980s. Her colorful murals can be found throughout Cuba. Her works contain women as a main theme, with intricate scenes that are both symbolic and subjective. Leal's art explores the subconscious and dreaming in a Surrealist and folkloric flavor.

Ramón Alejandro is a Cuban painter who was born in 1943. After living in exile in Paris for a time, he now lives in Miami, Florida. His artwork consists mostly of vividly colored surreal scenes of thematic landscapes.

Artists in Cuba continue to showcase their work on the city streets. Pictured here is a colorful modern mural in Havana.

TAINO CAVE PAINTINGS FOUND ON MONA ISLAND

In the cave systems of Mona Island near Puerto Rico, a large collection of rock art has been discovered by researchers from the United Kingdom and Puerto Rico who were exploring for signs of human life before Columbus arrived in the Americas. In these caves, scientists have found thousands of hand-drawn, -painted, and -scratched artwork on the cave walls.

Scientists estimate that humans arrived on Mona Island between 3000 and 2000 BCE. These people developed into the Taino culture that lived on the small island between the seventh and thirteenth centuries CE.

Images in the caves include depictions of animals, humans, and nature scenes. Scientists believe that these caves represented a kind of portal into a spiritual realm and that the artwork reflects facets of the early inhabitants' belief systems and cultural traditions. Some of the materials used for these paintings and drawings included charcoal and paint made from prepared plant gums, and some of the art was etched into the rock wall with a sharp tool.

The artwork on the cave walls of Mona Island are believed to have been drawn starting around 3000 BCE.

FESTIVE *PAPEL PICADO*: MEXICAN CUT PAPER DECORATIONS

Papel picado means "perforated paper"; it refers to a kind of Mexican folk art made out of very thin paper. The elaborate designs are often cut from colored tissue paper by using a drawn template and then pieces removed with small chisels. The tissue paper is layered so that the artist can

Papel picados are used as décor for holidays like Day of the Dead.

make as many as 40 *picados* at a time. Common themes include floral designs, skeletons, geometric shapes, or birds. *Papel picados* are used as party decorations and are hung up during both religious and secular festivities, such as baptisms, Christmas, Easter, birthday parties, and Day of the Dead.

Papel picados were used by the Aztecs. However, instead of the paper we use today, the Aztecs made paper from a kind of tree bark call *amatl*. They would cover the design on the paper with melted rubber and then paint on it.

This ancient Mayan mural depicts a performance by musicians found on the walls of Bonampak—an ancient Mayan archaeological site in Mexico.

MAYAN ART IN THE MAYAN CLASSICAL AGE

The 700 years of the Mayan Classic period (250–900 CE) saw a great flourishing of art. Although the humid climate has left few paintings intact, many examples of Mayan paintings can still be found in the walls, ceilings, and arches of temples. The scenes depict Mayan daily life, myths about the gods, battles, or stories of the elite. The Maya used several different colors of paint, especially red and black. Other colors used were yellow and a bright turquoise blue known as Maya blue.

Mayan artists came from all levels of society. Some were the elite—the children of government officials and royalty. Others were working commoners whose artistic passion and talent led them to their art. Still others practiced painting and drawing as a family business. It was customary for artists to sign their finished work in the event that it would catch the eye of nobility and be hired for further artwork. The Mayan rulers and nobility would commission works of art, such as a temple mural for public viewing, because they wanted to establish their status and prove their power.

GRAPHIC ART IN ARGENTINA

The history of graphic art in Argentina has generally reflected the social and economic policies of the country. Because of the many economic breakdowns and rampant inflation, Argentina has been a difficult place to hold a job as a designer. However, a number of pioneering graphic artists have been acknowledged in Argentinian society, and their work has become part of the university curriculum.

Hermenegildo Sábat, known by the pen name "Menchi," was a renowned Argentinian caricaturist born in Uruguay in 1933. His first drawing was published in the newspaper *El Pais* when he only 15 years old. His first job as a graphic artist was at the newspaper *Acción* in 1957. In time, his caricatures could be seen in periodicals such as *Crísis* and *Primera Plana*.

Joaquin Salvador Lavado, born in Mendoza, Argentina, in 1932, was known by the pen name "Quino." He dropped out of art school in 1949 because he grew tired of "drawing vases and plaster." Quino is best known for his successful comic strip *Mafalda*, which he began in 1964. In 1982 he was chosen as the Cartoonist of the Year by fellow cartoonists from around the world and has twice won the Konex Platinum Prize for Visual Arts.

Hermenegildo Sábat's portrait of Astor Piazzolla.

THE HAITIAN RENAISSANCE

The Modern movement in Haitian art that began in the 1940s is often referred to as the "Haitian Renaissance." It began with an American painter named DeWitt Peters, who taught painting at Le Centre d'Art in Port-au-Prince. The center provided exhibition space for 25 of Peters's students, and it increasingly attracted artists who were completely self-taught and painted in the "naïve" style of typical Haitian art.

Another factor that helped bring attention to the Haitian Renaissance was a visit to this island by the French Surrealist André Breton in 1945. Breton claimed that fellow Haitian artists were Surrealists, and he helped to promote Haitian artists in Europe and Latin America.

A "naïve" Haitian artist who gained recognition was Philomé Obin, who had already been painting scenes of everyday life since 1908. One of the most famous artists from Haiti was a vodou priest named Hector Hyppolite. He was noticed by DeWitt Peters because of his interesting artwork that was painted on the doors of a roadside bar aptly named "Ici la Renaissance."

Prosper Pierre-Louis was a Haitian artist that painted mystical vodou loas and spirits.

CHAPTER 5 MIDDLE EAST

The countries of the Middle East have long had a love affair with the art of the book. From the impeccable style of calligraphy in ancient illuminated texts to the beautiful, modern illustrations of children's books in Iran, drawing, painting, and the art of calligraphy continue to thrive throughout the Middle East.

قل هل يستوي الذين يعلمون والذين لا يعلمون

ISLAMIC CALLIGRAPHY

Calligraphy as a sophisticated art form is not unique to Islamic culture. The Japanese and Chinese have long used calligraphy and studied it as an art form, continuing to the present day. However, historically, the Islamic world used calligraphy in creative ways that were unknown to other cultures, and their written words went far beyond just writing with pen and paper.

The art of calligraphy can be considered one of the most fundamental components of Islamic art. Calligraphy has been used in the Islamic world not only for its aesthetic appeal but also as an underlying talismanic element. The Kufic style was the first formal style of calligraphy. Named after the city of Kufah in Iraq, it was used to write Koranic manuscripts. The embellishment of decorative ornamentation is common in Islamic calligraphy. For example, words can be written in a color other than black, such as gold. Words and letters may also be outlined or set against a background pattern. However, the decorations should never interfere or become a distraction from the sacred content of the text.

Calligraphers use size, colors, and styles of text to adorn a manuscript, but they must stick to certain rules of proportionality. The best calligraphers of the past were often employed within the ruler's palace or by the richest members of

Calligraphy was used to write Koranic manuscripts.

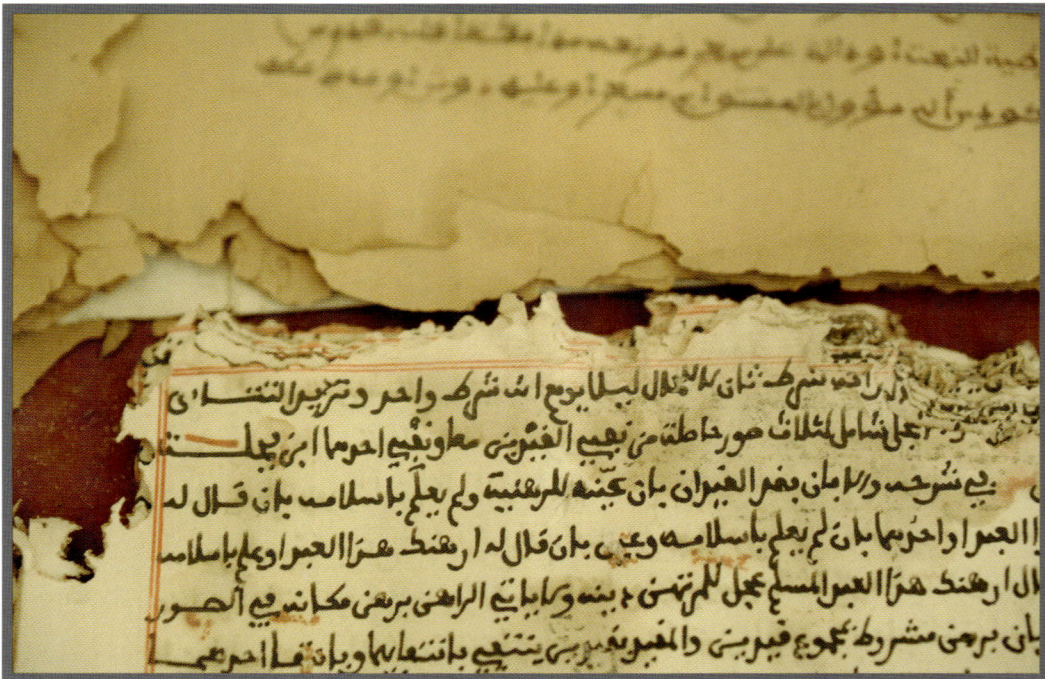

society, and they could command high commissions if they were very talented. It was often the calligrapher's job to write out the text first, and then they would work out the design, making sure that the lettering would fit in a well-balanced way. Once the calligraphic text was finished, other artists would add decorations and a rich binding for the book.

Designs by the best and most talented calligraphers were often retained so that they could be copied and studied by other calligraphers. These keepsakes were collected into albums to be appreciated by collectors and connoisseurs. Over time, some people began hanging some of these calligraphy samples on their walls, in the manner of a painting.

The materials used for calligraphy included the type of pen used, usually made from a reed. The nib of the pen was made by cutting the tip of the reed with a knife. The tip could be cut in different ways to create different effects for calligraphic decoration. Originally, calligraphy was written on vellum or parchment paper. Later, however, the paper was starched and polished to provide an exceedingly smooth surface for writing and embellishment.

Calligraphers were some of the most respected artists in Islamic society. Both men and women were calligraphers, and their status was based upon their talent and who they studied with. Training with a master could take many years, because the pupil had to learn to copy exactly from the model provided. These skills were passed down from master to apprentice for many generations.

A calligrapher writes tourists' names on paper in a Moroccan market.

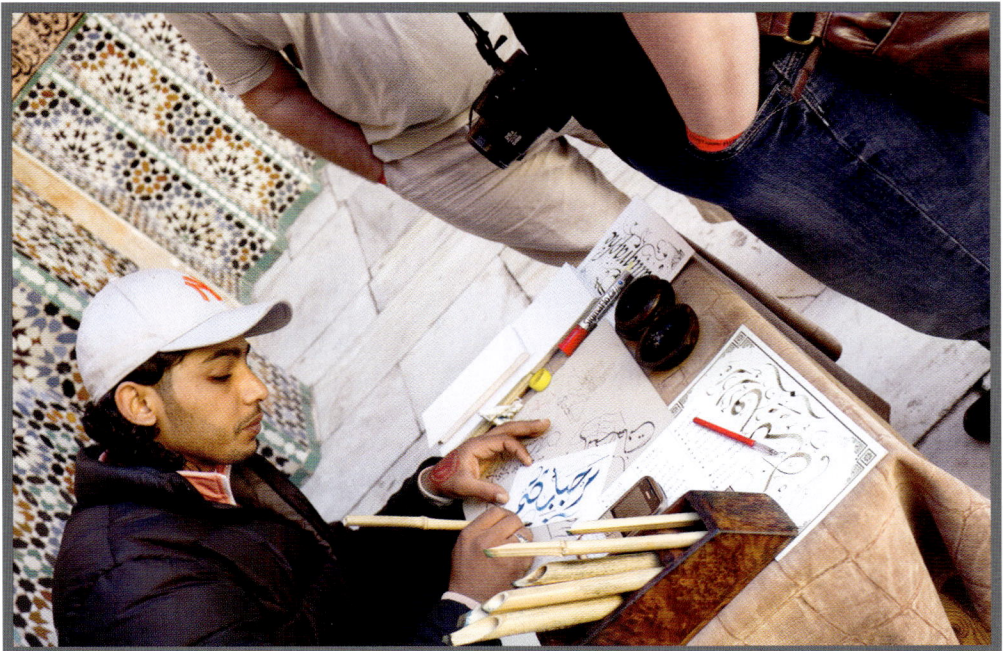

PERSIAN MINIATURE BOOK ILLUSTRATION

A Persian miniature is an ornately detailed painting done on a miniature scale, depicting a mythological or religious theme. The art of the Persian miniature spanned from the thirteenth to the sixteenth centuries but is still practiced today. Paintings can be a separate work or art, or they can be a part of a book illustration. These tiny paintings are highly detailed, with vivid colors, and they are created using a very small brush. However, they feature very complex scenes, often with accents in gold and silver leaf.

The Persian Empire had a rich history of court painting, but until the sixteenth century it was uncommon for artists to sign their artwork. The idea of Persian miniatures was probably borrowed from the Chinese, because some Chinese themes appear in very early versions of Persian miniatures.

A woman paints a traditional Persian miniature.

During the Ilkhanid period (1256–1353), the main center of production for miniatures was in Baghdad, Iraq, and Tabriz, in what is known today as Iran. Most Persian artists during this time worked at illustrating and illuminating books with religious and secular texts. Artists used highly decorative motifs that had Chinese influences such as peonies, lotuses, and dragons. The most famous artist of the day was Ahmad Musa, who was described as an artist who could "unveil the face of painting."

In the Jalairid period (1340–1411), the Jalairids ruled over western Persia. The books that were illustrated during this period were more tranquil and tended to focus on poetry, with subjects such as heroic accomplishments and great battles. A famous illustrator from the Jalairid period was Junayd, who was a pupil of Ahmad Musa.

The Safavid Dynasty (1501–1736) produced many decorative illustrated manuscripts in the Shirazi style, incorporating local traditions as well as borrowing elements from other Persian schools. These illuminations were divided into geometrically defined sections that were painted in bright colors.

Persian miniatures were originally commissioned as book illustrations for illuminated manuscripts. Some Persian miniatures could take up to a year to complete, and only the wealthiest people could afford to have them made. Over time, people began to collect these Persian miniatures as works of art, and they combined them together to create a book.

This Persian miniature is from "Shahnameh"—an epic poem written by Ferdowsi. The miniature depicts a battle between the armies of Faramarz and Mihark.

NEW HORIZONS ART AND ISRAELI ART THEMES

During the 1950s and 1960s, artists from Israel began to explore their own versions of the avant-garde art movement taking place in the United States and Europe. Immigrants arriving in Israel brought new trends and ideas that added to the flavor of the ongoing nationalism, Zionism, and socialism that were unique to Israel.

The "New Horizons" movement started with a group of artists that held an exhibition at the Habima National Theater in Tel Aviv in 1942. They called themselves "The Group of Eight." Members of this movement originally included Yehezkel Streichman, Avraham Natanson, Arie Aroch, Zvi Meirowitch, and Avigdor Stematsky. The group wanted to achieve a style that reflected their quest for Modernism mixed with Zionism, a variant of the European Modernist movement. Their works came away as an abstract style with a use of bright colors and bold brushstrokes.

Avigdor Stematsky poses with a piece of his artwork in the 1930s.

Although these abstract works of the New Horizon movement had a meaningful effect among art circles in Israel, it was nonetheless considered to be on the fringe and too explicit regarding the Zionist message. For example, Joseph Zaritsky, one of the leaders of the movement, produced a series of paintings called Yehiam, which featured Israeli kibbutzim. These paintings included a number of abstract Israeli landscapes.

Another New Horizons artist whose work was notable is Mordecai Ardon. His paintings often portray historical and mystical episodes from Jewish history, ranging from the Holocaust to biblical scenes. His painting *Gate of Light* (1953) shows the tree of life against a Surrealist landscape.

Israeli artists all have a unique way of expressing their art. However, they often used four common themes to express Israeli culture: interpretations of Jewish identity, the Israeli military, identity with the Hebrew language, and references to the Holocaust.

After the Israeli War of Independence in 1948, themes of war began to appear in Israeli artwork. These themes dealt mainly with the aftereffects of war, such as sadness and loss. Later, in the 1960s, artists such as David Reeb, Yoram Rozov, and Yigal Tumarkin shifted their focus from bereavement from past wars to political protest of Israeli soldiers and their treatment of the Palestinian people.

Since the twentieth century, the Hebrew alphabet has been used in drawing and painting as a way of visually expressing the Israeli identity. Israeli artists began to incorporate short texts of the Hebrew language into works of art and commercial designs. Artists such as Drora Domini, Hila Lulu-Lin, and Michael Sgan-Cohen all used Hebrew text in their artwork to represent idioms, proverbs, puns, and double meanings.

Until the 1980s, artistic interpretations of the Holocaust were very uncommon. Paintings that were created by Holocaust survivors in the 1960s and 1970s generally were not made public in art exhibitions. However, some Holocaust survivors did gain recognition with their abstract works, such as the Expressionistic drawings by Moshe Bernstein and Osias Hofstatter. The appearance of a Holocaust theme did not become prominent until the second generation of survivors, including Hayim Ma'or, began painting.

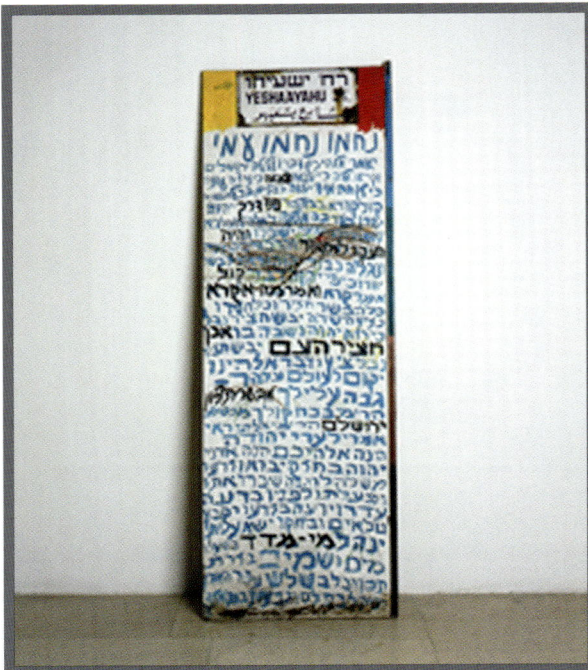

Michael Sgan-Cohen's Comfort Ye, Comfort Ye, My People.

BEZALEL: THE FIRST ART MOVEMENT OF ISRAEL

Israel is a land of historic and cultural significance for many people. At the turn of the nineteenth century, European Jews came to settle in Palestine. In 1906 the Bezalel Academy of Arts and Design was founded by the Jewish-Lithuanian artist Boris Schatz. The academy mixed traditional European styles of Art Nouveau with the Mediterranean and Palestinian influence of the area. By around 1910, the Bezalel Academy had grown in reputation, but the student artists began to rebel against the strictly European styles and traditions being taught. They sought out a new style that was distinctly "Israeli" and desired to return to their cultural roots of the time of King David and to incorporate more Middle Eastern flavor and motifs into their artwork. This new school of artists produced paintings and etchings that contained biblical themes and Jewish traditions that had a more Islamic design but was distinctly Israeli in identity.

Bezalel art.

THE SYMBOLISM OF PALESTINIAN "LIBERATION" ART

The Palestinian "liberation" art movement began in the 1960s with a small group of artists committed to establishing an art scene that showed the revolutionary struggle against the Israeli occupation. Their artwork depicted images of cultural pride and resistance with iconic symbolism. Today, traces of the liberation art movement can still be found in the paintings and drawings of young artists.

Liberation artists admired the Cubists and the Mexican Muralists. These Palestinian artists originally worked in a number of different mediums, and one of their goals was to have their work seen in every home and refugee tent. So, in addition to drawing and painting, artists made posters for mass distribution.

Liberation art makes use of symbolism to impart its message, implementing images of things that are popularly known in Palestinian life. For example, a horse symbolizes revolution, and a flute could mean the music of the resistance. The sun symbolizes freedom, and a gun with a dove means that peace will come after the fight for liberation. Artists also used the colors of the Palestinian flag, images of martyrs, village scenes, and prison bars or chains to represent their fight for freedom and peace.

Many liberation artists were activists and formed unions. They became socially responsible and encouraged younger artists to take up the cause of creating art for the liberation movement. One of the most prominent artists of Palestinian liberation art is Halaby, born in Jerusalem in 1936.

Many artists in Palestine have created their artwork on the wall that separates them from Israel.

His abstract art can be seen in public and private collections, including the Guggenheim Museum of Art in New York and the British Museum in London.

SYRIAN ARTISTS FIND A HOME IN LEBANON

Since civil war broke out in Syria in 2011, car bombings, shelling, and violence have brought the once energetic art scene in the country to a halt. Hundreds of Syrian artists have escaped to nearby Lebanon to seek refuge and continue their artwork. Splashes of paint on a canvas painted by Imad Habbab portray an explosion from the civil war in Syria. Habbab, originally from Damascus, described his intentions: "The explosion is about a moment that can erase all dreams, all opportunities, all ideas."

Syrian artists are finding their artwork is in demand because of their unique perspective on the reality of the problems in the Middle East. Lebanon has long been considered a center of culture, and it has provided many Syrian artists with a safe place to live and work. Another artist, Omar Ibrahim, from the southern As-Suwayda Province, portrays the plight of Syria in his artwork by painting bloody horses and hyenas. Ibrahim says that the animals are meant to symbolize the people and the government.

The devastation of Syria's civil war has led hundreds of Syrian artists to escape to nearby Lebanon where they are able to continue creating their art.

ANCIENT ROCK ART OF SAUDI ARABIA

The Kingdom of Saudi Arabia has more than 4,000 archaeological sites, and about 1,500 of them include rock art. Scientists believe that humans may have lived in this area up to 1 million years ago, but early examples of rock art date back from the Neolithic time period, around 12,000 BCE. At Jubbah, a very large carved panel was found that depicts masked women and men dancing, although it is possible that they are a representation of mythological figures with a horselike head and a human body. The rock art shows the group of dancers holding each other's hands in a dance that is similar to the way an *ardha* tribal dance is done today.

In almost all of the rock art found, the paintings can be dated back to between 10,000 and 7500 BCE. Most rock art features human figures with animals, especially dogs and cattle. Scientists think that these kinds of animals were domesticated and part of everyday life. In addition, many depictions of goddesses have been found in poses with their palms open and their fingers stretched out as they raise their hands. Hunting scenes are another common theme, but the animals are never wounded or pierced by an arrow. It is possible that these are magical illustrations symbolizing the continuance of animals as a food source. Some petroglyphs have even been found with inscriptions of people's names. One petroglyph with a name painted on it shows two women fighting, with a third women seemingly acting as a referee.

A petroglyph at Bir Hima—a rock art site in Saudi Arabia.

ANCIENT PAINTINGS OF ÇATALHÖYÜK

Çatalhöyük, in what is now South-Central Turkey, dates back more than 9,000 years and is one of the oldest preserved towns discovered by archaeologists. It has given scientists incredible insight into how ancient civilizations first formed into communities and towns. Çatalhöyük was inhabited for more than 2,000 years and had a population of up to 8,000 people. This ancient city contained no streets and comprised one gigantic building that was connected by separate, independent structures, with an opening in the ceiling that used a ladder for entry. The walls and ceiling of this settlement were supported by wood and brick, and people walked along the roof of each dwelling to get from place to place.

Inside each home, the people decorated their walls with paintings of their daily lives, such as hunting scenes, landscapes, wild animals, and ceremonies. There is evidence that these walls did not stay the same but were decorated over and over again every month or every season as the events in people's lives changed. This site is important because it provides scientists with information about how early hunter-gatherers began to form groups and settle into communities, and how art played an important role in their daily lives.

A hunting scene found inside of a Çatalhöyük home.

PERSIAN TIMURID ART

The Timurids belonged to a Turko–Mongol tribe in the Central Asian steppe. Their leader was named Timur, and he conquered most of Central Asia, Iraq, Iran, as well as parts of India and southern Russia. Timur enlisted artists and craftsmen from these conquered lands to create art in his capital of Samarkand, and his descendants continued to be leading patrons of Islamic art. Through this patronage, the Eastern Islamic world became a cultural center.

Some Timurid artists began to improve on the illustration of books by using paper rather than parchment. The illustrations of these book were noted for their use of elaborate calligraphy and rich colors. These illustrations were composed with more sense of space than previously used, enlisting simple concepts and bright colors. One of the most important works of this period is from around 1476. It contains the 155 miniatures of *Khavaran-nama (Book of the East)* by the artist Maulana Muhammad ibn Husam al-Din, a book of poems written about the legendary deeds of "Ali, the cousin and son-in-law of Muhammad." Other Timurid artists created wall paintings that depicted landscapes with Persian and Chinese styles of painting. Because most of the artists of this period came from other lands, the subject matter tended to vary significantly, but it eventually morphed into its own unique style that included wall paintings that featured the glorification of Timur.

A folio from the Book of the East.

QAJAR PAINTING

Traditional Qajar painting is believed to have begun during the Safavid Empire (1501–1722). The art of Qajar, which is located in present-day Iran, is most notable for its distinctive portraiture style. During this time, there was a heavy influence of Persian culture on the arts, and Qajar oil painting artists were inspired by European art movements of the time and by European masters such as Rembrandt and Rubens.

Some of the most famous works in Qajar paintings are the portraits of Persian shahs and other royalty, such as Fath Ali Shah Qajar (1797–1834). The artist would paint the royal subject in an elaborate style, with jewels, a velvet robe, and royal paraphernalia. The artist would also clarify the subject's level of royalty by painting a cartouche next to the subject's head that would signify his rank. Artists like Mihr 'Ali painted portraits where the features of the shah were emphasized, and the subject was posed in various manners, from a gentleman smelling flowers to an armor-clad warrior.

A painting of Fath Ali Shah by Mihr 'Ali.

CHAPTER 6 NORTH AMERICA

The paintings and drawings of North America encompass a wide range of styles, and the spirit of individuality is often used by artists to interpret their chosen medium. From native indigenous cave paintings and cultural and racial art movements to expressions of wonder regarding the American landscape, North American painters and illustrators have forged their way with a unique perspective.

CONTEMPORARY NATIVE AMERICAN PAINTING

The indigenous peoples of North America have been painting for as long as they have lived in tribes. They often painted symbols that had spiritual significance on items such as their tipi coverings, pottery, and even their horses. Native Americans are often considered a homogenous group rather than a complex and diverse collection of different communities and cultures. But Native Americans each offer an individual perspective in their artwork, reflecting not only their cultures and traditions but also their experiences as individuals.

Navajo sand painting is one example of Native American painting. In Navajo, the translation for sand painting means the "place where the gods come and go." Sand paintings are used for healing and religious ceremonies by tribal shamans, but after the ceremony, the sand painting is always destroyed. In the 1940s, the Navajo decided that they wanted to preserve sand painting as an art, so they slightly altered their designs to avoid being sacrilegious. Sand paintings are made by slowly pouring sand made from crushed stone and minerals over a wooden board. It takes great skill to be an accomplished sand painter, and Navajo sand painting can be quite expensive to purchase.

Navajos use sand painting during healing and religious ceremonies.

In addition to sand painting, the Navajo people painted on the walls of caves.

Many Native American artists, such as R. C. Gorman and Oscar Howe, helped to close the gap between mainstream art and Native American art. The contemporary artist Frank Buffalo Hyde is a Nez Perce and Onondaga. He is a visual artist who rejects the Native American stereotypes that are commonly associated with "Indian" artists. Hyde's work is a combination of street art, whimsical Surrealism, and fantastic colors. Hyde claims that he is still searching for his voice, but his main aim is to hold up a mirror to popular society.

Duane Slick has both Winnebago and Fox ancestry, and he primarily works with shadows and monochromatic colors. His paintings feature an attempt to understand Native peoples beyond the trapped-in history of mainstream society. Slick has claimed that he was inspired by the "laughter of the coyote, the eternal trickster and ultimate survivor, that saturated and filled our daily lives."

Shonto Begay is an established Diné artist who paints with pointillistic dots, a lyrical representation of marks that "repeat like the words of a Navajo prayer." Begay's work is poignant and accessible. His Impressionistic images reflect the struggles and hardships of Native Americans. They can often be dark and call to mind the harsher realities of alcohol, poverty, and drug abuse.

THE BIRTH OF THE SUPER-HERO: COMIC BOOK ART

Comic books have been popular in America since the early 1800s. They started out as political and satirical cartoons printed in magazines and newspapers. One of the earliest cartoonists of this period was Thomas Nast, whose critical drawings played a large part in bringing down a corrupt political New York leader named William M. "Boss" Tweed in 1870.

The first comic book is widely considered to be *The Yellow Kid in McFadden's Flats*, published in 1897. This comic book featured reprints of comic strips in black and white. As the form gained popularity, other comic books started to be published, including *Buster Brown*, *Mutt & Jeff*, *The Katzenjammer Kids*, and *Happy Hooligan*, as well as a monthly comic book titled *Comic Monthly*, which began publication in 1922. In 1933 the first comic book in color, *Funnies on Parade*, was published. The first completely original comic book was published by National Allied Publications in 1935. It was called *New Fun* and was illustrated and written by Jerry Siegel and Joe Shuster, the creators of Superman.

The so-called Golden Age of Comic Books started around 1938 with the publication of Superman in *Action Comics #1* and Batman about a year later. The success of these comic books was followed up with a flurry of activity by Marvel Comics's predecessor, with superheroes that featured secret identities, colorful costumes, and superpowers. By 1940, Timely Publications had introduced characters such as Human Torch, Prince Namor the Sub-Mariner, and Angel. Fawcett Comics featured Green Lantern, Captain Marvel, and Wonder Woman.

Between 1938 and the mid-1940s, comic books were so in demand that publishers had monthly sales of over 100,000 copies for popular characters. Batman, Captain Marvel, and Superman comics regularly sold about 1.5 million copies per

The Yellow Kid in McFadden's Flats *is considered to be the first comic book.*

month in the early 1940s. Some famous comic book illustrators include the following:

Steve Ditko: A partner of writer Marvel Comics's creator Stan Lee, Ditko helped create characters such as Spider-Man, Dr. Strange, Hulk, and Iron Man. Ditko used bold colors and drew his characters with strength and energy. After a falling out with Stan Lee, he moved to work at the rival company, DC Comics.

Frank Frazetta: Born in Brooklyn, New York, Frazetta began his comic book illustration career at age 16 when he got a job doing pencil clean-ups at the comic artist Bernard Baily's studio. Frazetta was soon creating his own drawings in many different comic genres, such as fantasy, mystery, westerns, and funny animals. Frazetta worked on Li'l Abner and Flash Gordon, and he is well known for his paintings and book cover illustrations.

Jack Kirby: Kirby was born in New York City in 1917. He was nicknamed the "King of Comics" and is notable for creating characters such as the Fantastic Four, X-Men, Black Panther, and Thor during the Golden Age of Comic Books.

Steve Ditko's first published comic book cover was The Thing *#12.*

The Unsung Art of Magazine Covers

American magazine cover design has evolved into a kind of creative artwork since the Golden Age of American Illustration between 1880 and 1960. Advances in printing technology, an abundant supply of inexpensive paper, and mass mailing led to the meteoric rise of new magazines for the masses. Publishers commissioned first-rate artists to create artwork that would appeal to and visually communicate with their audiences.

Artists such as James Preston, Howard Pyle, Norman Rockwell, Georges Lepape, N.C. Wyeth, Helen Dryden, Ruth Ford Harper, and many others created works that were worthy of an art museum. The illustrations on the covers of these magazines conveyed important messages about their time, and they represent a snapshot of American society. National icons such as James Montgomery Flagg's self-portrait of himself as Uncle Sam exclaiming "I Want You" became embedded in the American lexicon.

PAINTERS OF THE HARLEM RENAISSANCE

From the 1920s to the 1930s, a flurry of artistic and intellectual creativity among African Americans occurred in art and became known as the "Harlem Renaissance." In New York City at the time, the Harlem neighborhood began to attract a stylish and prosperous middle class that desired to celebrate their African heritage and culture. Artists of the Harlem Renaissance had a desire to change their stereotype of a denigrated character into a new, respectable identity. Black artists borrowed cultural models and inspiration from Africa. Many black Americans went to study art in Europe, but as the Great Depression began, these artists had to return to America to continue their work.

One of Archibald J. Motley's self-portraits.

The art of the Harlem Renaissance often featured an Expressionistic style with bold colors. Artists such as Palmer C. Hayden portrayed African American subjects in the joy of their everyday life, such as dancing, making music, or eating. In the 1930s, New York City became an art hot spot with the opening of new museums, galleries, and art schools, such as the Museum of Modern Art, which was opened in 1929.

One Renaissance artist, Aaron Douglas (1898–1979), painted murals and created illustrations for many black magazines, such as *Opportunity* and *The Crisis*. Douglas was sponsored by the WPA (Works Progress Administration) to complete a mural for the 135th Street branch of the New York Public Library in Harlem, which is now known as the Schomburg Center for Research in Black Culture. It is a four-panel series called *Aspects of Negro Life*. The mural depicts the journey of

African Americans, from being taken into slavery from Africa to life in the United States to freedom after the Civil War to living everyday life in the modern city.

Archibald J. Motley was a popular Harlem Renaissance artist who also chose subjects that featured African Americans enjoying culture in an attempt to break down black stereotypes. His 1929 painting titled *Blues* shows a group of African Americans celebrating music and dance. The Harlem Renaissance artist Lois Mailou Jones was born at the height of prejudice and racial discrimination, although she attended the School of the Museum of Fine Arts in Boston. Jones entered art competitions by getting her white friends to hand in her submissions. Her paintings have been featured in *Ebony* magazine.

William Henry Johnson's Three Friends.

One of the most celebrated artists of the Harlem Renaissance was William Henry Johnson. His work covered many different genres, but he is best known for his use of textures in an Expressionistic folk style. His painting subjects included portraits, scenes of everyday life, and landscapes.

EL MOVIMIENTO: THE CHICANO ART MOVEMENT

The Chicano art movement, or *El Movimiento*, began in the 1960s and was an attempt by Mexican American artists to establish an individual identity that coincided with cultural, political, and social issues. It was a movement to resist the racial stereotypes and social norms that prevented Chicano cultural autonomy. The Chicano art movement used art to express cultural values, protest inequality, and unify Chicanos by using art as a way to share culture and history.

One of the unifying principles of this art movement was a term known as *Chicanismo*. *Chicanismo* was a way for Chicanos to reclaim their past and future identities by depicting Chicano histories and narratives through artworks and murals. One event that took place in the 1960s was to rename the Southwestern United States as Aztlan, which signified the spiritual land of the Chicanos.

The Chicano art movement continued in the 1970s, with artists who were committed to serving in their communities and reinforcing the concept of cultural identity. Artists created posters, murals, and billboard art, and they held art exhibitions that focused on Chicano unification at galleries in their communities. Images of this time depicted reinventions of the Mexican Mural movement and works by artists such as Diego Rivera, Frida Kahlo, and graphic artist José Guadalupe Posada. They also created artwork with indigenous themes of symbolism and pre-Columbian art.

Jose Guadalupe Posada's Grand Electric Skull.

THE WHIMSICAL FOLK ART OF RURAL AMERICA

Throughout history, people living in rural areas often made objects by hand, learning on their own or watching someone else pass down their artistic skills. Until the late nineteenth century, most American homes contained artwork painted by local artists or artists who traveled from town to town and painted on commission. Many of these artists did not have any formal artistic training. The "folk art" paintings they created were creative and whimsical, and some offered political or social messages. Most of these artists are unknown, although it is sometimes possible to tell what community the painting may have come from.

One common theme in folk art during this time period was to have a family portrait painted, either of an individual family member or the whole family. Other themes reflected everyday life, as in *Plantation Dance* (c. 1785–1795), a watercolor by John Rose, who was a plantation owner in South Carolina. This painting depicts slaves playing musical instruments and dancing. Itinerate artists such as Samuel Addison Shute (1803–1836) and Ruth Whittier Shute (1803–1882) traveled from town to town in search of work on commission. One such work is *Master Burnham*, a portrait of a child done in gouache and watercolor, with pencil and ink. The child's colorful clothes, with his playful dog and vivid flowers, create an interesting image with unusual anatomical proportions. On some level, contemporary folk art lives on through the artists who sell their crafts on Web sites like etsy.com.

John Rose's Plantation Dance.

AMERICAN ALBUM ART

The term *album* originally referred to a 78-rpm shellac music disc that was wrapped in a paper sleeve and housed in a leather book with a front and a spine. In the 1930s, artists such as Alex Steinweiss started illustrating the covers of these albums for singers like Paul Robeson or on classical records recorded by major symphony orchestras. These album illustrations led to bigger sales, but the real change came when the 78-rpm album was converted to a long-playing 33-1/3 rpm record, also called an LP.

Because record companies wanted to avoid damage to these LPs, they started using a folded-over board format to house the record. This new format provided a lot of room for artistic experimentation, and album illustrators were given license to create imaginative and artistic artwork on the LP covers.

One of the first album covers to attract popular attention was an album design for Capitol Records for *The King Cole Trio*. This collection of four 78-rpm records featured an abstract image with a guitar, a double bass, and a piano keyboard underneath a golden crown. After topping the *Billboard* Best Selling Popular Record Albums chart and reaching number one with many singles from the album, other record companies were ready to incorporate album art as a selling tool to popularize their recording artists. Many famous artists, such as Roger Dean, Burt Goldblatt, and Andy Warhol, started their careers by designing album covers.

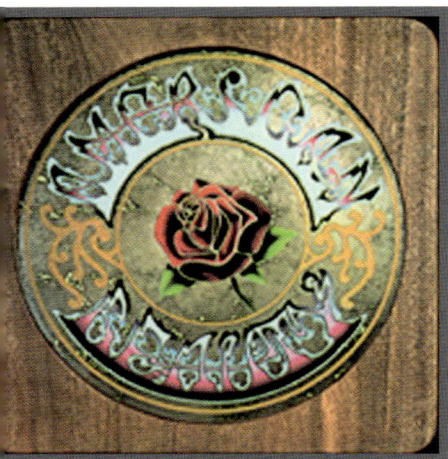

The Grateful Dead turned to Stanley "Mouse" Miller to design their album cover for American Beauty.

Many famous covers are from the postwar jazz and bebop musical era. Jim Flor, who went to school at the Chicago Art Academy, worked at RCA Victor's art department in the 1950s and helped to illustrate a distinctive style with a blend of Surrealism and caricature. His cover illustrations featured exaggerated characters with Picasso-like juxtaposed eyes, and he came up with monthly creations that are considered masterpieces. S. Neil Fujita, a Hawaiian-born graphic designer, worked at Columbia Records from 1954 to 1960. Fujita designed covers for jazz artists such as Art Blakey, Miles Davis, and Charles Mingus. His style for album cover designs incorporated the style and techniques of Modern art influences such as Paul Klee and Picasso.

By the 1960s, artists and graphic designers such as Stanley "Mouse" Miller and Alton Kelley were illustrating albums for the San Francisco psychedelic music scene. Bands like the Grateful Dead used Mouse Miller's artistic talent to design and illustrate albums such as *American Beauty*, which featured a painting of a red rose with iconic lettering on a wooden background.

THE ROCK ART OF THE CUMBERLAND PLATEAU

Rock art paintings are scattered around the caves and bluffs of the Cumberland Plateau and have been there for centuries. They were painted by the ancestors of the indigenous tribes of the American Southeast. Scientists think that all of this cave art is part of a pattern that is interrelated with how these ancient rock artists saw the universe and what their place was within it. The collection of caves on the Cumberland Plateau span an area from Northern Alabama to the Kentucky borderline. Many of the paintings are between 500 and 900 years old, but one painting of a hunter located in East-Central Tennessee has been radiocarbon dated to 6,000 years ago.

Many of the Cumberland Plateau cave paintings are drawn in red, a color that symbolized life.

All of the examples of cave art in the Cumberland Plateau share common themes in color and subjects. There are 94 sites in total (so far), with 50 located underground. Many of the works are drawn in red, a color that symbolized life, and also face south and west.

Scientists think that the cave artists were watchful of celestial phenomena and believed that the universe was layered—with an "upper world" where the stars, sun, and moon influenced human life on earth; a "middle world" where humans lived; and a "lower world" that other, darker beings inhabited. The images on the outside of caves are of human with their hands and feet in an extended position. They have very long fingers, as if they are trying to reach out of the rock. Inside the caves, the images tend to be much darker in nature, with images of supernatural serpents and dogs accompanied by humans. These images are thought to be associated with death, danger, and transformation. Still other images feature humans flying or show tiny birds with wings.

THE GROUP OF SEVEN: CANADA'S LANDSCAPE ARTISTS

The Group of Seven were Canadian landscape painters who gathered themselves together in 1920. The seven original members were Frederick Varley, Lawren Harris, Frank Johnston, Arthur Lismer, A. Y. Jackson, J. E. H. MacDonald, and Franklin Carmichael. Carmichael, Johnston, Varley, Lismer, and MacDonald all met at a design firm in Toronto called Grip Limited. Lismer befriended Jackson and Harris at an Arts and Letters Club in Toronto. The group split during World War I, but they later rejoined and began to travel around Ontario to sketch and paint landscapes.

The Group of Seven was greatly influenced by the Impressionist movement. They had their first exhibition in 1920. Their work was characterized by decorative and rich colors that were applied in a thick, impasto style. They were considered pioneers of Canadian art and were known for their Impressionistic landscape scenes. They had their last show in 1931 and broke up the Group of Seven to form a new group called The Canadian Group of Painters.

Gas Chamber at Seaford *by Frederick Varley.*

PAINTERS OF THE ASHCAN SCHOOL

The Ashcan school of painting was known for its urban and gritty subject matter, which incorporated gestural brushwork and a dark and muted palette. Heavily influenced by the painter Robert Henri, the Ashcan school comprised a group of artists based in New York City who believed in the worthiness of working-class life and the immigrant diaspora. Other artists in the group included George Luks, William Glackens, John Sloan, and George Bellows. They sought to depict art that was not an elitist ideal, but rather the real and honest work of everyday working people and their families.

Ashcan artists rejected the idea of American Impressionism, with its emphasis on peaceful and pleasing idylls. They preferred to focus on the dynamic energy of authenticity and on the realness of one's first impression. They aimed to create a sense of beauty from extraordinary yet ordinary working people. Ashcan artists painted scenes of New York City, such as people walking in the park, laundry hanging from a fire escape, and prostitutes working the street.

Robert Henri's Snow in New York.

Artists of the Ashcan school had backgrounds as newspaper illustrators. They rejected the skillful drawing and rendering of the earlier Impressionists and chose to use quick brushstrokes with a sketchy quality to capture the energy of the moment.

ARON OF KANGEQ: GREENLAND'S INUIT PAINTER

Aron of Kangeq was an Inuit painter born in Greenland in 1822. His watercolors depicted his native Inuit culture and history and the sometimes bloody encounters that his people experienced with the Danish colonizers. His work was first discovered by Danish explorers who anchored in Greenland because of bad weather. They happened to collect a number of watercolor paintings among other artworks that had been created in response to an initiative by Hinrich Rink, a Danish geologist and the administrator of South Greenland, who became interested in trying to preserve the oral traditions and stories of the Inuit people. Rink decided to publish these Inuit folktales, and he used Aron of Kangeq's illustrations in each of the books that were made.

Although a skilled hunter, Aron of Kangeq became ill with tuberculosis and was no longer able to go hunting or out in a kayak. As a way to help keep busy, he began to record the old traditions and folklore of his people by drawing and using watercolors. He created about 160 watercolors in total.

Aron's Tupilak, Woman and Man.

CHAPTER ⑦ OCEANIA

Australia and New Zealand's ancient aboriginal history dates back at least 60,000 years. Oceania's drawing and painting culture is part of a complex story of ancestral mythology and traditions mixed with "the walkabout" of European settlers who came to explore this new country and paint images of their new home.

NEW ZEALAND EXPLORER ART

When Europeans began arriving in New Zealand, they immediately set out to record the people and places of the land. Exploration ships were commissioned to find possible areas for future colonies, and they often included an artist to document the journey and illustrate new findings. One of the first European artworks created was made by Isaac Gilsemans, who made the drawing during an expedition in 1642.

The first drawings that explorer artists made of the Maori people were created in 1769 by Sir Joseph Banks and Sydney Parkinson, who accompanied Captain James Cook on his ship, the *Endeavour*. In the following years, other artists captured new discoveries of flora and fauna, and they sparked the imagination of Europeans who viewed their work of this new land. Cook's artists also created paintings and descriptions of traditional Moko tattoos, which led to tattoos becoming a tradition of the British Navy.

Other explorer artists included Sydney Parkinson, James Webber, and William Hodges, who all made numerous drawings during expeditions made by Cook. Hodges in particular was a skillful oil painter as well as draughtsman.

Isaac Gilsemans's drawing of the Maori people.

Hodges's Resolution and Adventure with Fishing Craft in Matavai Bay *portrays the two ships of Commander James Cook's second voyage in the Pacific.*

Later expeditions included French artists such as Louis de Sainson, who traveled on the *Astrolabe* in 1827 with Dumont d'Urville to draw works of the Bay of Islands. Dumont d'Urville later traveled again with the artist L. Le Breton to explore the east coast of the South Island, including Otago Harbor and the Weller whaling station.

Interest grew in hiring artists to paint the New Zealand landscape, because plans were made by the New Zealand Company to colonize the country. A small group of surveyors who were also artists were hired by the company to survey the land and sketch possible sites for homes, which were published in *Residences in Various Parts of New Zealand* (1842). Among these artists hired was Charles Heaphy, a talented artist who went on to paint *Hokianga*, a painting of a timber cutting that portrayed the vast wonder of the New Zealand landscape.

MOKO: MAORI TATTOO ART

The indigenous people of New Zealand are called the Maori. Their form of body art is a tattooing process called *Moko*. *Moko* is considered highly sacred by the Maori, and the practice is thought to have been originally brought to New Zealand from Polynesia. To the Maori people, the head is considered to be the most sacred part of the body. Facial tattoos are common, consisting of spiral patterns and curved shapes. Facial *Moko*, which can cover the whole face, is used as a symbol of social standing and power.

Maori tattoos are highly individualized, and none are like another. The tattoos are considered a rite of passage that involves a ritual and usually begins at the beginning of adolescence. A Maori tattoo artist, called a *tohunga*, is a highly respected member of the community. The *tohunga* is generally a man, but some women also practice the art. Before the *tohunga* begins work on tattooing a face, he studies the shape of the face very carefully to decide what designs and symbols would look best.

One legend that explains the origin of Maori tattoos suggests that the practice of *Moko* came from the underworld, called Uetonga. In the legend, a young warrior named Mataora falls in love with the princess of the underworld, named Niwareka.

In Maori culture, the head is considered to be the most sacred part of the body; therefore, Moko facial tattoos are the most common.

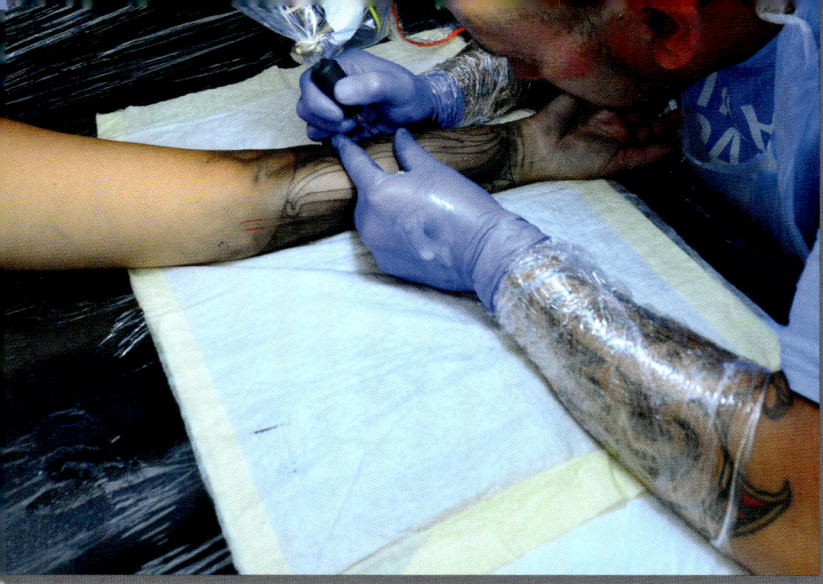

Although Moko tattoo artists traditionally use chisels and knives, they will sometimes use modern needle equipment.

The princess Niwareka decides to come aboveground to marry Mataora. But Mataora is unkind to his new wife, so she returns to the underworld. Mataora is so sorry for his actions that he goes back to the underworld and try to win Niwareka back. When he reaches the underworld, Niwareka's relatives laugh at him and make fun of him, but Mataora apologizes for his unkind behavior anyway. Niwareka forgives her husband, and her father gives Mataora the gift of the art of *Moko* so that he can bring it back to his people to learn.

Traditional *Moko* tattooing generally does not use needles. Instead, the Maori use chisels and knives made from sharp stones, bone, or shark teeth. The chisel, called an *uhi*, is made from albatross bone. Nowadays, *Moko* tattooing is sometimes done with modern machines. The ink that is used for the tattoos comes from naturally made ingredients. Black pigments are created by using burnt wood. Lighter pigments come from caterpillars that are infected with a special fungus or a kind of gum mixed with animal fat.

Australian Aboriginal Symbols and Their Meanings

Because Australian aboriginal people have no written language, they often use symbols and icons to interpret their stories and traditions to pass on to the next generation. Symbols vary from region to region. Most of the aboriginal symbols are relatively simple, but they become more complex messages when combined with other symbols. For example, the shape of a U is used for the symbol of a man, but if the U is placed next to concentric circles and spiral lines, then it would mean that "a waterman" is magically calling the rain.

AUSTRALIAN IMPRESSIONISM: THE HEIDELBERG SCHOOL

At the end of the nineteenth century, it was common for Australian artists to visit to London, the largest city in the world at that time. Artists who had studied at the National Gallery School in Melbourne, such as Arthur Streeton, Charles Douglas Richardson, and Tom Roberts, traveled to London and Paris with the ambition of establishing their careers and emulating new ideas in the art world.

These artists brought back with them the influence of other European Naturalist painters, such as Jules Bastien-Lepage, and used this style in their landscape painting. Upon their return to Australia, Arthur Streeton and other artists pursued their painting amid a bohemian lifestyle, traveling to various pastoral landscapes to paint the untainted countryside before the development of cities could take away the natural beauty of the land.

The "Heidelberg School" was coined as a term by the art critic Sidney Dickinson in 1891 after reviewing works by the artists Walter Withers and Arthur

Frederick McCubbin's The Pioneer.

A plein air landscape by Louis Buvelot.

Streeton, who had traveled with other artists to paint *en plein air* in Heidelberg outside of the city of Melbourne. Other key figures of the Heidelberg School were Tom Roberts, Frederick McCubbin, and Charles Conder, as well as Withers and Streeton. This movement was later described as Australian Impressionism.

The Heidelberg School artists got together in "artist camps" to paint the countryside, drawing on the Impressionist and Naturalist ideas that they had taken away from Europe. They sought to capture the natural beauty of the Australian bush and the intense sunlight. The Heidelberg School's first exhibition was in 1889; it was called the 9 x 5 Impression Exhibition and featured McCubbin, Streeton, Conder, and Roberts, among others. The exhibition consisted of small, nine-inch by five-inch sketches painted on wood from cigar boxes. It was the first art exhibition that was considered distinctly Australian.

However, Australian Impressionism had little in common with the French Impressionism movement in Europe, or with artists such as Claude Monet and Camille Pissarro, whose focus was on the vibration of light and color. Australia was too far away to be affected by happenings in Europe, and most artists from Australia were going back to London, not Paris.

THE SECRET ART OF ABORIGINAL DOT PAINTING

Dot paintings originated around 1971. An art teacher named Geoffrey Bardon was assigned to teach aboriginal children art. He noticed that some of the aboriginal elders would draw designs in the sand as they told stories. Intrigued, Bardon assigned his students a project to paint something based on their traditional culture of Dreamtime mythology. The paintings drew interest from the community, and soon some of the men began to paint their designs on pieces of cardboard and wood.

These paintings are a unique kind of art that is a distinctive Australian Aboriginal art form. From the outside, the simple dot style of these Aboriginal paintings is beautiful on its own, but they have a more hidden meaning as well, which comes with a deeper intention. Underneath these dots lies the sacred meaning of the culture and traditions of the aboriginal people.

Traditionally, during ceremonies, the aboriginal people drew their sacred designs on the ground after smoothing out a place on the soil. These designs were outlined with a series of circles and dots. Only the people who participated in the ceremony saw these designs, because the soil that they were written on would be smoothed over at the end of the ceremony.

This practice was not possible with painting, so Aboriginal artists had to come up with a different way to express their culture through painting and drawing without exposing the meaning of their sacred symbols to Western influences. So they abstracted their artwork with dots to disguise the sacred designs and keep their real meaning secret.

Originally, the colors of these dot paintings were restricted to white, black, red, and yellow, colors that were made from pipe clay, ocher, and charcoal. Later, acrylic paints were used to allow for a wider range of colors and more vivid hues. The artworks feature dots, spirals, lines and dashes, cross-hatching, and maps of circles that are composed of the pictorial language of the aboriginal people.

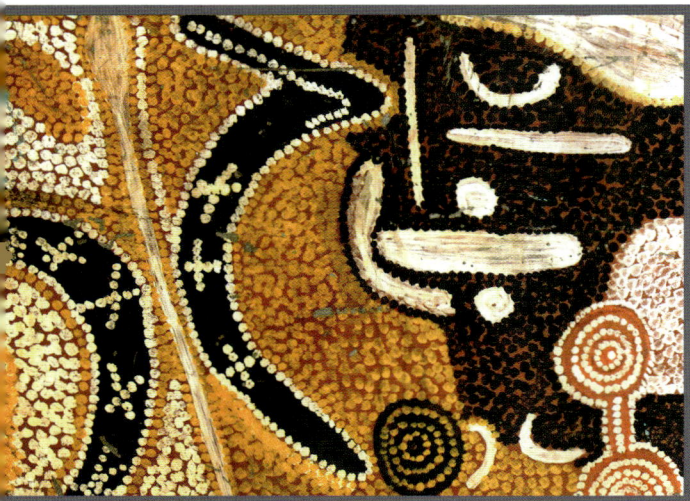

Dot art expresses Aboriginal culture through painting without exposing the meaning of sacred symbols to Western influences.

ROCK ART OF KAKADU NATIONAL PARK

Kakadu National Park has perhaps the most examples of rock art in the world. There are around 5,000 aboriginal sites that include rock art, ceremonial ocher, and shelters with painted walls. Some sites date back more than 50,000 years.

The rock shelters of Ubirr in Kakadu's northeast contain paintings of fish and animals such as catfish, mullet, turtles, wallabies, and possums—animals that aboriginal families hunted as they moved from place to place. Other paintings in Kakadu National Park contain depictions of the first contact with "whitefellas" that are believed to be the buffalo hunters around the 1880s.

Another painting nearby shows a depiction of the Namarrgarn Sisters, who are evil spirits that live in the stars and can make people get sick with a magical string. One of the oldest paintings, a Rainbow Serpent known as *Garranga'rrelito*, is more than 23,000 years old. At Anbangang, there is a painting of a Lightning Man, a Dreamtime ancestor who controls the lightning in storms during the wet season.

According to a myth from Dreamtime, Mimi spirits were the first to paint on these rocks, and they passed on their stories and knowledge to the aboriginal peoples of the land. It is believed that the ancestral spirits sometimes enter the rock paintings, making them sacred dreaming places.

The word for Aboriginal rock art is *gunbim*. Aboriginal rock art was painted for many reasons, including that paintings could be created only by people who had the right knowledge; for example, magical paintings could be painted only by people who had the knowledge of that specific magic.

The paints for Aboriginal rock art were made out of pigments that were crushed on a stone palette and then mixed with water into a kind of paste. Art brushes were made from human hair, feather, or reeds. Sometimes the painters would blow the paint onto the wall by spitting the paint out of their mouth to make a stencil. One example of this technique is the hand stencils at Nanguluwur and Ubirr. The majority of the oldest paintings are all in red because the hematite (a reddish iron oxide) can last a very long time.

The Aboriginal rock art of Kakadu National Park.

MODERN AUSTRALIAN ART MOVEMENTS

At the beginning of Australian settlement in 1788, most art was dominated by landscape painting. In the 1930s, a Modernist movement began to take place that had a tendency to favor *plein air* painting with a naturalistic tone. By the end of the 1980s, many artists in Australia had moved from a theme of post–Modernism to subjects that were more distinctive of international themes, such as globalization, global warming, and decolonization. This new movement gained the attention of international art markets and put Australia on the map of contemporary art.

One such artist that is gaining attention is Reka One, originally known as James Reka. With influences in cartoons and pop culture, Reka One's style melds together a mix of high and low art. He takes his experiences in graphic design and his love for street art to create large–scale mural paintings. These creations are dream-like, with much attention paid to the detail work and choice of color scheme in a mix of surreal and abstract exploration.

Another noteworthy artist is Ben Quilty, who won the Doug Moran National Portrait Prize in 2009. In 2011 he was the official war artist in Afghanistan. His paintings often use thick layers of paint and blocks of color to depict dark and morose subjects. His own experiences with drugs and alcohol assist him in getting deep into the subject of his paintings, as can be seen in his haunting portraits of soldiers and his series of Rorschach paintings.

Artist Ben Quilty with one of his pieces at an exhibition in London.

AUSTRALIA'S COLONIAL ART PERIOD

The Australian colonial period ranged from 1788 to around 1880, before Australia changed from New South Wales to a Commonwealth. Artists from this period were either immigrants from Britain or the next generation to be born in Australia. They were primarily influenced by French and English landscape painting and used watercolors to paint, although commercial opportunities for these artists were limited because art was not viewed as being relevant during this time period.

The earliest settlements in Australia were the convict settlements in Sydney. But there were also settlers who came to pan for gold, and other colonialists came to settle into a new life in Australia after the post-Napoleonic depression. One of these settlers was John Glover (1767–1849), who was already a successful English landscape artist and teacher. He settled himself into a country home in Tasmania and began to paint the landscape of his new homeland. Glover eventually acquired a circle of other watercolorists who also enjoyed landscape painting. Among them was Francis Guillemard Simpkinson de Wesselow, an accomplished artist and naval officer who created a number of landscape paintings around Van Diemen's Land (Tasmania). Some of Simpkinson's paintings were included in the first public exhibition held in Australia, on January 6, 1845.

John Glover's Natives on the Ouse River, Van Diemen's Land.

AUSTRALIAN ABORIGINAL ART

The first aboriginals are believed to have settled in Australia between 60,000 and 80,000 years ago. Rock art made from ocher has been found from aboriginal people dating back 20,000 years. Because Australian aboriginals have no written language, culture and stories are passed down by using symbols and icons in their artwork.

Aboriginal art is centered on storytelling, and although these indigenous people have been using body paint and ocher for cave painting for thousands of years, it was not until the 1930s that they began to paint on canvas as a formal form of artwork.

One of the first exhibitions by an Aboriginal artist was in 1937 by Albert Namatjira. It was a collection of watercolor landscapes, and other Aboriginal artists also primarily used watercolors as a medium until the 1970s. Since then, Aboriginal art has become an exciting contemporary form of art. Artists such as Gordon Bennett, Emily Kame Kngwarreye, Paddy Bedford, Rover Thomas, and Clifford Possum have paved the way for future Aboriginal artists to interpret their collective knowledge of culture and traditions by using dots, gestural paint strokes, and blocks of color.

The Rainbow Serpent at Dualgur *by Rover Thomas.*

GAUGIN'S LOVE AFFAIR WITH TAHITI

Inspired by Pierre Loti's novel *Le Mariage de Loti* (1880), Paul Gauguin traveled to Papeete, Tahiti, in 1891 with a romantic image of the island being an untouched paradise. Upon his arrival, he was disappointed by the level of colonialization by the French, and he vowed to immerse himself in Tahitian culture. For example, he used Tahitian titles for his works, such as *Manao Tupapau* (1892), which means "The Spirit of the Dead Watching." Gauguin also used idealized island landscapes against an ocean backdrop in order to further remove himself from conventional Western thinking.

Gauguin's painting style changed significantly during his time in Tahiti. His work changed from flattened imagery to a kind of "primitivism," with round, fluid brush-strokes and tonally harmonic lines. One example of this new style can be seen in *Where Do We Come From? What Are We? Where Are We Going?* (1897). This work represents a dreamlike contemplation of the life cycle, beginning with an infant and ending in an image of a very old woman.

In July 1893, Gauguin went back to France, thinking that his paintings from Tahiti would bring him the fame and fortune he had long been craving. But after his illustrated woodcuts were published in a book called *Noa* and a one-man exhibition of his works was held, he met with little interest or income and decided to return to Tahiti, where he remained for the rest of his life.

Gauguin's Where Do We Come From? What Are We? Where Are We Going?

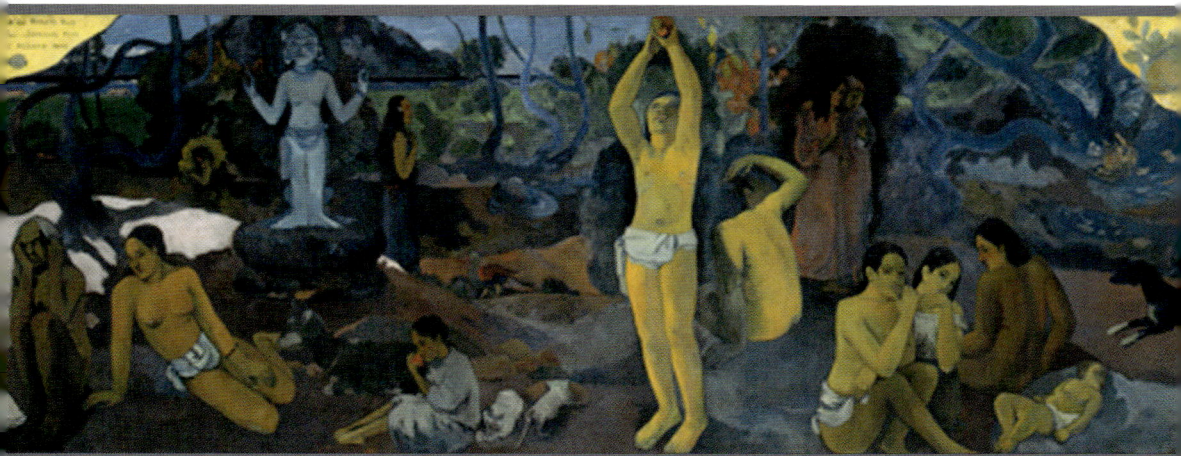

BODY PAINTING IN PAPUA, NEW GUINEA

Body painting is a kind of decoration that is common among the indigenous tribes in Papua, New Guinea, and it plays a big role in their culture. It is associated with festivals and important celebrations that are used to as a way to distinguish different tribes. To these tribes, their body is a canvas that is waiting to be painted and decorated with ornaments. It is used as a way to bridge the connection between the earthly world and the spirit world. In the Wahgi tribe, body painting is used during the marriage ceremony. The participants of the tribe paint their bodies in colors of white, red, and yellow. Nowadays, synthetic paint is used, but originally the paint was made with ingredients from nature.

Papua, New Guinea, has over 800 different ethnic groups, and many of them practice a form of traditional body art. Each tribe has a unique way to make their body paints, and each practices this cultural decoration for various reasons. For example, the Chimbu tribe did not make contact with the Western world until 1934. They practice a kind of body art that includes painting themselves in the form of a black-and-white skeleton. This form of body painting was originally intended to intimidate enemies. In recent times, it is part of a celebration called "Sing," where different clans in the tribe get together and practice the traditions of their culture.

The Chimbu tribe often paints their bodies to resemble a black-and white-skeleton.

FURTHER READING & INTERNET RESOURCES

BOOKS

Ganz, Nicholas. *Graffiti World: Street Art from Five Continents* Updated ed. Edited by Tristan Manco. New York: Harry N. Abrams, 2009.
A collection of more than 2,000 illustrations that features 150 street artists who work in a variety of mediums.

Gombrich, Ernst Hans. *The Story of Art.* 16th ed. New York: Phaidon Press, 1995.
Gain a better understanding of art history in an easy-to-read format with this well-rounded book that contains numerous full-color illustrations and fold-out pages.

Gompertz, Will. *What Are You Looking At?: The Surprising, Shocking, and Sometimes Strange Story of 150 Years of Modern Art.* Reprint. New York: Plume, 2013.
The former director of Tate Gallery in London takes the reader on an artful ride, showing the reader how to look at and understand modern art.

Lewis, Samella. *African American Art and Artists.* Berkeley: University of California Press, 2003.
A look at the lives and works of African American artists from the 1800s to the present.

Stokstad, Marilyn, and Michael W. Cothren. *Art History.* 6th Ed. Upper Saddle River, NJ: Pearson, 2017.
A fresh perspective on art history from knowledgeable authors. This book makes a great reference for students or art lovers.

WEB SITES

www.oxfordartonline.com/page/timelines-of-world-art. This site, "Timelines of World Art," includes art from all over the world, so you can search and learn about significant moments in art history.

www.metmuseum.org/art/collection/. The Metropolitan Museum's art collection can be searched, so you can get a close-up look at your favorite artist or learn something new about an art movement from history.

www.khanacademy.org/humanities/art-history. The Khan Academy's online art history course goes from art history basics to the art of Oceania.

www.oxfordartonline.com/page/women-in-the-visual-arts. Although women have participated in drawing and painting since ancient times, they are still underrepresented in the mainstream art world. This article on "Women in the Visual Arts" provides a look at some women who made a big impact in the world of art.

http://collection.folkartmuseum.org/collections/591/paintings/objects. Explore this interesting and whimsical collection of folk art paintings from the 1700s to modern times, from the Folk Art Museum.

www.illustrationhistory.org. Discover the artists and history of illustration at the Norman Rockwell Museum. From children's book illustrators in the Golden Age of Illustration to the pulp illustrators of romance novels, this Web site has lots of interesting history and images to explore.

www.moma.org/collection/. Search online for over 70,000 works of modern art from contemporary artists on the Web site for the Museum of Modern Art. From Andy Warhol to Roy Lichtenstein, this museum in New York City has an evolving collection of new and interesting artworks.

INDEX

AUTHOR'S BIOGRAPHY

Christina Wedberg is a freelance writer and illustrator who lives in Brooklyn, New York. She mainly writes and illustrates fiction for children and young adults. She also designs and illustrates products for her stores on Zazzle.com and Amazon.com. She has a certificate in children's illustration from the London Art College, is a member of Society of Children's Book Writers and Illustrators, and is a winner of a college scholarship from the National League of American Pen Women (NLAPW).

CREDITS

COVER

(clockwise from top left) Persian miniature, steve estvanik/Shutterstock; mural by Diego Rivera, National Palace, Mexico City, Mexico, Wing Travelling/Dreamstime; painting by Marc Chagall, Marc Chagall Museum, Nice, France, Joe Sohm/Dreamstime; petroglyph, Newspaper Rock, Utah, Jason P Ross/Dreamstime; *The Siesta* by Paul Gauguin, Everett-Art/Shutterstock; Manga café, Kyoto, Japan, Hai Huy Ton That/Dreamstime

INTERIOR

1, Olga Zinovskaya/Dreamstime; 2–3, Zoltan Tarlacz/Dreamstime; 5, Dmitry Rukhlenko/Shutterstock; 9, Zzayko/Dreamstime; 10, Vladimir Melnik/Dreamstime; 11, Spiroview Inc./Dreamstime; 12, Luisa Puccini/Shutterstock; 13, Luisa Puccini/Shutterstock; 14, Wikimedia Commons; 15, Bettina Strenske/Newscom; 16, Askme9/Dreamstime; 17, Askme9/Dreamstime; 18, helovi/iStock; 19, jackmalipan/iStock; 20, Piero Cruciatti/Newscom; 21, Fine Art Images/Newscom; 22, Pierre-Yves Babelon/Shutterstock; 23, Attila Jandi/Shutterstock; 24, Danilo Mongiello/Dreamstime; 25, Sahua/Dreamstime; 26, Jing Hao/Wikimedia Commons; 27, Max421/Dreamstime; 28, Lewis Tse Pui Lung/Shutterstock; 29, Julioaldana/Dreamstime; 30, Kobby Dagan/Shutterstock; 31, Cropbot/Wikimedia Commons; 32, Biserko/Dreamstime; 33, ben bryant/Shutterstock; 34, AtomicSparkle/iStock; 35, Cherdchai Chaivimol/Dreamstime; 36, Boonsom/Dreamstime; 37, Shin Yun-bok/Wikimedia Commons; 38, Chrisukphoto/Dreamstime; 39, Dreamsidhe/Dreamstime; 40, isogood/iStock; 41, sedmak/iStock; 42, Martini314/Dreamstime; 43, Ivan Varyukhin/Dreamstime; 44, Anne Vallayer-Coster/Wikimedia Commons; 45, Fede Galizia/Wikimedia Commons; 47, Francisco Goya/Wikimedia Commons; 48, Marc Chagall/Wikimedia Commons; 49, Wrangel/Dreamstime; 50 (UP), PKM/Wikimedia Commons; 50 (LO), peuceta/iStock; 51, Marsana/Dreamstime; 52, Hel080808/Dreamstime; 53, Gamemon/Dreamstime; 54, Album / Fine Art Images/Newscom; 55, Zoltan Tarlacz/Dreamstime; 56, Rainer Lesniewski/iStock; 57, karlagarviav/iStock; 58, Evelyn Sampaio/iStock; 59, FernandoPodolski/iStock; 60, James R. Martin/Shutterstock; 61, narvikk/iStock; 62, Lucian Milasan/Dreamstime; 63, Serge Aucoin/Wikimedia Commons; 64 (UP), Carlos Ivan Palacios/Shutterstock; 64 (LO), Jacob Rus/Wikimedia Commons; 65, Barcex/Wikimedia Commons; 66, Jakemathai/Wikimedia Commons; 67, Adel Mohamady/Dreamstime; 68, Quick Shot/Shutterstock; 69, numbeos/iStock; 70, MehmetO/Shutterstock; 71, steve estvanik/Shutterstock; 72, Talmoryair/Wikimedia Commons; 73, Michael Sgan-Cohen/Wikimedia Commons; 74, Ephraim Moses Lilien/Wikimedia Commons; 75, badahos/Shutterstock; 76, Smallcreativeunit5/Dreamstime; 77, retlaw snellac/Wikimedia Commons; 78, Laudibi/Dreamstime; 79, Maulana Muhammad Ibn Husam ad Din/Wikimedia Commons; 80, Wikimedia Commons; 81, rudall30/Shutterstock; 82, Edward S. Curtis/Wikimedia Commons; 83, Konoplytska/iStock; 84, Richard Felton Outcault/Wikimedia Commons; 85, Steve Ditko/Wikimedia Commons; 86, Alexisrael/Wikimedia Commons; 87, William Johnson/Wikimedia Commons; 88, José Guadalupe Posada/Wikimedia Commons; 89, John Rose/Wikimedia Commons; 90, Wikimedia Commons; 91, Alexey Stiop/Shutterstock; 92, Frederick Varley/Wikimedia Commons; 93, Robert Henri/Wikimedia Commons; 94, Aron of Kangeq/Wikimedia Commons; 95, AKV/Shutterstock; 96, Isaack Gilsemans/Wikimedia Commons; 97, William Hodges/Wikimedia Commons; 98, ChameleonsEye/Shutterstock; 99, Rafael Ben Ari/Dreamstime; 100, Frederick McCubbin/Wikimedia Commons; 101, Louis Buvelot/Wikimedia Commons; 102, Inge Hogenbijl/Dreamstime; 103, JohnCrux/iStock; 104, Bettina Strenske/Newscom; 105, John Glover/Wikimedia Commons; 106, akg-Images/Newscom; 107, Paul Gauguin/Wikimedia Commons; 108, JohnCrux/iStock